Kristan's fingers stroked Jennifer's back, beginning at her shoulders and slowly moving downward, then eased her back against the couch. Her tongue traveled down and under Jennifer's breast, tracing a warm path to her belly where she stopped at the top of her jeans.

"I want to taste everywhere." Kristan's voice smoked with desire. She slowly unzipped Jennifer's jeans. Her tongue followed the slow movement of the zipper downward. She hesitated when she saw the red lace bikini panties that matched the bra. "This is like opening a magnificently wrapped gift," she said. Her tongue stroked the skin just above the coarse curly hair, then she kissed her way back up Jennifer's belly, then to her breasts. She sucked first one and then the other. She touched the outside of Jennifer's jeans and Jennifer arched her body against Kristan's hand.

Visit

Bella Books

at

BellaBooks.com

or call our toll-free number

1-800-729-4992

The Way Life Should Be

Diana Tremain Braund

Bella
BOOKS

2004

Bella Books, Inc.
P.O. Box 10543
Tallahassee, FL 32302

First published 1998 by Naiad Press

Printed in the United States of America on acid-free paper
First Edition, Second Printing - January 2005

Editor: Christi Cassidy
Cover designer: Sandy Knowles

ISBN 1-931513-66-X

To Lee
who wields a great red pen,
tells me the truth
and keeps me out of trouble,

and

to Heather
who gave me insight
into a mother's daily life.

Chapter 1

Before the deaths, Kristan Cassidy always loved springtime in Maine the best. For her it was the only season that counted. It was the moment of new breath, of life awakening to the rays of the sun reaching out for a blue sky that won't end. It was like making love to a lusty and passionate woman. You bury your face in her breasts, nearly suffocate in her scent and know that what will follow will be one hell of a pleasure.

There is also the equinox sky, deep blue with large cumulus clouds that float lazily above. You tolerate the spring rains because afterwards you don't have to shovel. Spring storms turn the sky angry and black and the clouds dissolve into long fingers that sometimes reach down and touch the water.

Seasoned Maine eyes, used to the spring sky, search easterly for that first calm before the Nor'easter that will rip through trees, slash power lines and batter 100-year-old houses that sigh wearily as they stand hard against yet another gale.

Spring is that period when the landscape's grays and tans that recently reigned turn vibrant green. Antique cars, hidden in winter garages, away from the winter salt that eats at their undersides, are rolled out into the sunlight, washed and placed back on the road.

Desires and expressions of love that lay dormant all winter, too cold and tired to germinate, explode and the entire countryside erupts. And the memories that we clung to since the fall, that danced along the edges of death and decay, are reborn and there is new dimension to old thoughts.

The people who live here are Downeasters, people whose hard *R*s become *A*s. People with nicknames like Bunky and Boomba. They embrace their Down East heritage because it recalls a time when three- and four-masted ships sailed north out of Boston harbor and caught the easterly wind that pushed them along the Maine coast.

It is Monday and it is April.

Kristan Cassidy eased her gray Subaru onto the country road. She looked left to Globe Cove. "I'll never get tired of looking at that," she mumbled to herself through her morning sleepiness. It was early. The multi-colored lobster boats—deep reds, bright blues, grass greens—eased up and down in the tiny swells. She was headed to the office after a long weekend of work. She ran her hand through her curly blond hair and pushed it back from her forehead.

"It's a great morning, guys," WHJL's morning disc jockey, Bill Haines, announced.

"Yeah, for you, twit," she said to the radio.

"Let's do a goldie oldie. Does anyone say that anymore?" Haines asked. "Here's the King. I wonder what he would have been like had he lived?" he asked his unseen audience. "Elvis—'I Didn't Love You the Way I Should Have.'"

Kristan turned up the radio. The song nagged at the edges of her memory. It pushed heavily at the steel fireproof door she kept locked on a former love, a love she had screwed up. "Best left shut," she said aloud. Although the past was locked, she held her breath as she thought about the firm body tight against hers, arms around her waist, lips touching.

Stop that, she mentally scolded herself. Celibacy, she had come to believe, was best, although it could be a real cuticle-chewer.

She stopped at the stop sign and let the few morning cars go by, eased in behind a 1957 Chevrolet, then passed the slowpoke. She ignored the solid yellow line indicating that it was not a passing zone. She waved to Mrs. McCurdy, who apparently was headed into Bailey's Cove.

Kristan mulled over her schedule. Morning court and then cop-shop briefing. She reminded herself that she needed to call the port director to find out how many bids they had for construction of the new port. That might be a story, especially if nobody had bid on the project. She also needed to see the city manager. It had been a while since they'd had coffee. Time to catch up on city gossip.

The scanner crackled. Kristan turned down the radio and turned up the scanner that was hooked to the underside of her dash.

"We have a report of a ten-forty-five at the Karl P. Crowley residence on Tremont Road." Although the voice offered no name, Kristan knew it was Billy Wakefield, a dispatcher with the Regional Communication Center at the sheriff's department. "I repeat, we have a report of a ten-forty-five at the Karl P. Crowley residence on Tremont Road."

"Ten-four," another voice said. "My E.T.A. ten minutes." It was Officer Joey Miller.

Kristan sighed. Crowley must have been pounding on his wife again. What a nice respite it would be if she pounded on him for a change.

There were certain crimes she did not bother to chase, and this was one of them. It would only be a news story if he killed her.

Impoverished, with high alcohol and drug-abuse rates, Jefferson County was populated with husbands who pounded on their wives, girlfriends and children. Periodically, sociologists, hell-bent on getting their Ph.D.s, headed Down East to study the population and cases of abuse. They would publish their papers, compare the county with Appalachia, even draw parallels between the two areas claiming

3

that both held similarly inbred people. Solutions proposed were always the same: raise the economic level, educate the riffraff, encourage the women to just say no and walk. The Ph.D.s would shoot out their statistics with a shotgun, taking aim at nothing more than their dissertation committee's members, who would nod approvingly.

The scanner crackled again.

"Situation under control. Subject has left the house," Officer Miller intoned in that clipped scanner- voice so familiar to Kristan.

"Ten-four," the R.C.C. dispatcher answered.

"Should we notify Spruce Haven?"

"Negative," the officer answered. "Victim says she will stay here."

Kristan thought about Spruce Haven and its safe houses for women. They were temporary shelters, but most women eventually returned home. She laughed to herself. If Clara Crowley had agreed to leave her home, that would have been a news story.

Kristan followed Route 1, past the Quoddy Inn Motel run by her friends Susan Tackach and Angela Clark. It was early spring and business at the motel still was light. Tourists usually didn't discover the Down East area until well into June. She drove past the bridge that connected Bailey's Cove with Canada.

The smaller stores in Bailey's Cove were just beginning to open. There were cars in the Wal-Mart lot, but they were workers, not shoppers. Kristan drove past the Main Street Shopping Center and toward the wharf. Her favorite restaurant, Tippys, would be packed with locals eating and sharing gossip.

She pulled in next to Toby's new Chevrolet Bronco. They had a date for breakfast.

When Kristan opened the screen door that separated her from the laughter inside the small diner, everyone sitting on the red vinyl-covered stainless steel stools at the counter turned to see who had entered. It was not unusual for the locals to give a fisheye to new-comers. She waved to several of the town officials. Johnny Collins, community development director, was there, his pudgy little body hunched over two eggs and bacon, pushing the food in like a steam shovel. He was with two lobstermen who already had been out in their boats to tend to their traps.

She scanned the main room looking for Toby and caught sight of him at the back table. She smiled to herself as she crossed the room and tried to imagine what it was like to be a stranger walking into this place. The scrutiny, the watchful eyes, the question marks about who you were must be discomforting.

Most tourists who wandered in never returned. There was a rite of passage connected with Tippys. You had to be born in Bailey's Cove or have lived there for at least ten years before people stopped staring. Summer people and tourists didn't qualify.

For the most part, restaurants Down East represented fried-food heaven. Tippy had run the eatery forever. Kristan remembered her father talking about going there as a young man. The only difference was that Tip moved slower these days, his 70 years weighing heavily on his feet. She could see him through the faded green grease-spotted curtain that separated the kitchen from the main room. The smell of fried fish permeated the curtains and walls.

Kristan was glad Toby had chosen one of the better booths; at least the seats weren't split or the tabletop spotted from cigarettes carelessly dropped from ashtrays. She knew she would have to run the gauntlet of regulars, people she had to stop and banter with.

"Mayor, councilors." She nodded to Mayor Jasper Green and two of the city's six councilors. She grinned at City Manager Sally Ingersoll and reached over and tapped the police chief on the shoulder. "Bad mood?" she asked Joey Ramsdell.

"No," he grumbled.

"You must be talking about budgets," Kristan teased. She leaned over, patting his shoulders, covered by the familiar dark blue of his uniform. She winked at the city manager. "Come on, ask her nice and she'll give you the new police cruiser."

"He can ask ten times nice, and I won't be able to push that through the city council," Sally said. At six feet, Sally towered over most people, including the chief, even when she was sitting. She cupped her coffee mug in two hands and bent to sip what probably was her fifteenth that morning.

Kristan reached over and gently punched Joe in the arm. "Hang tough."

"Just to let you know, we arrested somebody you know for driving to endanger."

"Who?" Kristan asked.

"David Robinson. His buddy Jerald McCormick was with him. Someday Robinson is going to kill somebody with that souped-up car he drives."

Kristan shook her head. "I hope not. Remember that time he nearly ran me off the road? I was coming back from a meeting. The sucker just laughed."

"How about taking away his license?" Sally asked the chief.

"We have. His license was yanked once, but a few months later he applied to the state and got it back. Someday he is going to do something that will get that license lifted forever."

"Hopefully he won't kill anyone in the process." Kristan looked across the room and saw an impatient Toby waiting for her. "Gotta go." She nodded to several others as she crossed the room.

"Hey, liked your piece on the dragonflies," Bobby Winston, owner of the local radio station and Toby's boss, yelled across the room to her. Bobby and his wife, Marge, had breakfast at Tippys almost every morning.

"Thanks," she yelled back as she slid into the seat across from Toby.

He nodded toward the assembly of people Kristan had spoken with. "You should run for office."

"Why?"

"You'd do well. You got the political shmoozing down pat."

Kristan laughed. "I guess it does look like that, but you never know when you're going to need a quotable quote," she said as she studied the menu. "You ignore somebody, they get hurt feelings, but you know that."

Toby worked as a part-time news director. The rest of the time he filled in on the air. On Saturday and Sunday nights he produced a golden oldies show that was popular with the over-forty group. Although he was good at gathering news he didn't share Kristan's drive for getting the story. His first love was music.

Theresa Madsen, five months pregnant, was at her elbow in seconds. Kristan grinned; she liked the attention. "The usual?"

"Uh hum," Kristan answered. "How is baby Madsen doing?"

"Going to be a field-goal kicker." Theresa rubbed her hand against her stomach. "God, if I knew it was going to be this uncomfortable I never would have gotten pregnant," she groused.

Kristan laughed. "Come on, Theresa, you and Carl have been trying for years."

"Ayuh." Theresa grinned. "It's just this kicking part that's so damned uncomfortable."

"Hey, can we have more coffee over here?" two of the fishermen yelled from across the room.

"Hold your bait, I'll be there," she yelled back. Theresa grinned and winked at Kristan before she walked away.

"What's doing?" Toby asked Kristan.

"Not much," she said.

"If you're not busy this weekend, I was thinking of taking the boat over to Bayport," Toby said. "Thought we could catch a bite and maybe ride over to the Old Sow and then to St. Andrews."

The Old Sow was one of the largest tidal whirlpools in the Western Hemisphere and a favorite of Kristan's. It appears three hours before high tide and was surrounded by smaller whirlpools called the Old Sow's piglets. The patient observer was rewarded with a fountain that rose several feet into the air at the center of the whirlpool. There were reports of boats that had disappeared into the Old Sow, but there was no wreckage to confirm those Down East tales.

"I'd love to. I'm off this weekend," she said.

Kristan and Toby were easy with each other. He had that weathered tan look that remained even in the dead of winter. Respected and well liked, he was familiar to everyone with his slow-moving humor and earnest concern for the community.

He had left town after high school to attend Maine Broadcast School, and after graduation he worked at a number of radio stations around the country. At forty, he had returned to Bailey's Cove and was content with his small-town popularity.

Kristan had gone to the University of Maine, but she returned immediately after graduation when she landed a job with the local weekly. Later she was hired as a reporter for the daily newspaper.

Theresa returned with steaming hot blueberry muffins and a glass of milk. She set a bowl of whipped butter in front of Kristan. "God, I'll never be able to eat all those," Kristan groaned.

"He will," Theresa said.

Toby grinned and patted his stomach. "This is starting to grow faster than yours."

Theresa sniffed. "Well, at least mine will be gone in another four months."

Kristan split one of the steaming blueberry muffins in half. Wild blueberries are indigenous to Maine and juicier than the domestic varieties grown elsewhere. She spread on a dollop of whipped butter. She liked to watch the deep blue juice and yellow commingle. "I love these." She took a large bite. Butter dripped on her chin and she grabbed a napkin.

Toby pushed aside his messy plate of what had been bacon and eggs and reached for a muffin.

The door slammed, and Kristan forced herself to resist the urge to turn around and gawk.

"It's Francis. He has a woman with him," Toby said. "Nice-looking woman."

Kristan grinned. "Let's see, for you to have an appreciative eye, she has to be tall, at least five-seven, with black willowy hair and flat-chested, with the build of one of those anorexic models you see in glamour magazines."

"My God, you've described her to a T. How did you know?"

"Because that's your type." Kristan sniffed knowingly.

"They are coming this way," he warned.

Kristan put her muffin down. She frowned because she hated to be seated in a booth when she had to talk with someone. It gave the person who was standing an edge.

Kristan guessed the woman was the new assistant district attorney. Two weeks earlier the D.A. had told Kristan about his new employee. She eavesdropped as Francis introduced the mystery woman to the city manager and the police chief and knew she had pegged her right.

"Wipe your chin," Toby said.

Kristan hastily scrubbed a napkin across her chin.

"These here," Francis said as he walked up to their table, "are our local rag reporters."

"Thanks, Francis. See if I help get you elected next time." Kristan grinned. She was startled that the woman bore no resemblance to the woman she had described to Toby. She was small, with long wavy hair, intensely dark brown eyes, gorgeous long eyelashes and a handshake that could strangle a seagull. Definitely not skinny; definitely well-endowed.

"Kristan Cassidy, meet Assistant District Attorney Jennifer Ogden," Francis said.

"Pleased to meet you," Kristan said. Toby gave Kristan a cat-that-swallowed-the-canary grin. He had hoodwinked her, and he knew she knew it.

"This is Toby March, he works for the radio station over on Water Street. You usually can see these two together," Francis told Jennifer as she shook Toby's hand.

"I've heard a lot about you," Jennifer said to Kristan.

Kristan was struck by Jennifer's unwavering eye contact. "Believe me, I am not going to repeat that cliché and say, 'I hope it wasn't all bad.' " Kristan grinned. "But I suspect if you were listening to this old legal eagle, you didn't hear much that was good."

"Scoot over," Francis said as he pushed Kristan. Kristan slid across the seat. Toby stepped aside to allow Jennifer into the booth.

Kristan watched as Jennifer arranged her navy blue skirt. A gold indistinguishable amulet hung from a chain on her neck. It rested against a light-blue silky blouse that contrasted sharply with the dark navy jacket.

"Would you like a blueberry muffin?" Kristan asked Jennifer. Francis was already eyeing the plate.

"Thanks." Jennifer took one of the napkins from the finger-printed metal holder and reached for Kristan's knife. "May I?" There was something seductive about the move.

"Sure. Would you like coffee?"

"Of course we'd like coffee," Francis answered. He twisted his short bulky frame around in the seat and caught Theresa's eye. "Hey, darlin', a couple of coffees over here." Kristan leaned over and picked a piece of muffin out of Francis's graying beard. "Thanks." He reached across Kristan to the box of napkins and grabbed one.

"Are you here permanently?" Toby asked Jennifer.

Kristan smiled to herself. She knew Toby was drooling inside.

"I have to return to Portland for a couple of weeks, to close out some of my cases and transfer others. Then I'll pack for the big move."

"I don't envy you," Kristan said.

"I'm turning several cases over to her," Francis said between mouthfuls. "Jennifer is an experienced prosecutor, and she won some big cases in Portland."

"Coffee?" Theresa asked Jennifer and Francis. They nodded.

"Portland. Most folks move from here to there. You know, city versus rural, culture versus backwoods. There's more than just distance between the two worlds," Toby said.

Jennifer laughed. "It's really not mysterious. I inherited my grandmother's home, and I decided I could do with some rural surroundings. The house is just off Route One in Cranberry Bluffs. Actually, I spent a few summers here when I was growing up, so I know the area. When this job opened up, I applied."

"And I was smart enough to snatch her up," Francis said smugly.

"Usually we get either new graduates, fresh from law school," Kristan said, "or old men with one foot in retirement."

"Well, I've been out of law school for several years, and I haven't begun to think about retirement yet." Jennifer smiled.

"Well, welcome, but watch out for this curmudgeon." Kristan jabbed Francis with her elbow. "He tends to get into trouble with the media. He loves the female television types. They come up here with their Barbie doll brains and painful cuteness, and he just melts. I love their interview question. 'Oh, Francis, please tell me what a bad man is,'" Kristan said in a breathy Marilyn Monroe voice. "They turn on the camera, he gets that deer-in-the-headlights look and says, 'A bad man is one of those naughty people who do bad things to people.'" Kristan put on a deep male voice. "End of interview."

Jennifer laughed.

"You're full of it," Francis said good-naturedly. "She's just jealous because they scoop her every time."

"Scoop me!" Kristan said with mocked injury. "They can't even find this county unless there's murder and mayhem." Kristan felt her beeper vibrate against her hip. It was her office. "Sorry, I've got to leave."

Francis dropped his muffin and licked his fingers, then slid out of the booth, a tough move for a man whose belly washed over his belt.

"Nice meeting you," Kristan said to Jennifer. "We can talk shop later," she said to Toby. "Don't eat all the muffins," she chided Francis.

Kristan dropped some money on the counter, winked at Theresa and walked out of the diner.

Chapter 2

The trip out of the diner had been just as yakky as the trip in, and Kristan sighed as she eased back into the Subaru. She liked small-town living and especially this small town. It had 5,000 people, just enough to make it a city, but small enough to feel like people cared. There was one theater, but it had three screens, so the latest movies were always playing. Latest by Maine standards, not L.A.'s. There were two car dealers, a few clothing, hardware and furniture stores, six churches and plenty of fast-food restaurants. Of course, there was no shortage of bars.

Kristan's office was located between two law offices across from the courthouse. She parked in front and saw that the mail was over-flowing the black box attached to the wall next to her door. She picked up the latest edition of the paper that had been thrown in front of the entryway by the papergirl.

Her message box told her she had six calls. She pushed the play-back; the tape whirred, then beeped. The first message was from the dentist's office reminding her of her tooth-filling appointment. The second was from her assignment editor, Jerry Delaney. Apparently when he couldn't reach her at the office, he had beeped her. The other messages were easy callbacks, people with information about news stories or upcoming meetings. She jotted down their names and numbers on the pad she kept on her desk.

First she dialed the toll-free number that connected her with the Bangor office. It was seconds by telephone, two hours by car. She liked that kind of distance—the editors were there, an ever-present nuisance, but not close enough to micromanage her time.

As a field reporter, she and all the other field reporters once had been trusted decision-makers. But a year ago, the publisher hired new executive editor Bill Torrey, and editorial decisions now were made in Bangor. The exec had been the food editor of a large metropolitan newspaper. Kristan wondered at his journalistic judgment. Another reporter had complained that he wouldn't know a news story if it jumped up and bit him in the nose.

"Jerry Delaney," the voice said in her ear.

"You rang?"

"Yes, have you filed your budget yet?" The budget was a synopsis of the news stories a reporter would cover that day.

"Not yet, but I have an hour." Kristan wondered at the call. He usually didn't bug her about her budget because she always made the ten a.m. deadline. She waited for him to get to the real reason for the call.

Jerry had been with the paper for thirty-five years, first as a reporter, later as the paper's senior writer. When Bill Torrey revamped and eliminated his job as specialty reporter, he was made an assignment editor.

"What are you filing today?"

"I'll be in Superior Court most of the day."

"Yeah, yeah, I remember now."

"Anyway, that's where I'll be."

13

"Good. I want you to scout out more features. There are some big picture stories down there that we want, people doing things," he said. "Court stuff is important, but we need the other things too."

Kristan stared at her bulletin board. Now she understood the reason for the call. She had watched as the paper had slowly changed from hard and local news to features. The front page, once reserved for hard-hitting stuff, now showcased magazine-style puff pieces that should have shown up in the feature section. They were running out of fluff, she thought.

Kristan sighed. "I am still looking." She knew it was decision time—jump on the elevator or get off and do something else. "I promise, I am looking around, but with Harry's retirement, I'm frazzled trying to stay on top of the breaking stories."

Harry had shared reportorial duties with Kristan, working the southern half of the county. When he retired, the paper had promised a replacement, but a year had passed and she was still alone.

"Look, Bill wants more features, so give me a list by the end of the week."

"Sure." Kristan smiled. Jerry couldn't remember where he had hung his coat that morning, so she knew the one-week deadline wouldn't matter. The telephone clicked in her ear; he never said good-bye.

Kristan sighed again. She had to be in court in thirty minutes. She stopped and looked at the time. She and Tina were supposed to have lunch. She reached for the telephone but decided against it. She picked up copies of a letter of recommendation she had written for her friend Tina and dashed to her car. Tina was hoping to get a job as an elementary-school teacher's aide and Kristan had agreed to help.

Chapter 3

Tina answered her soft rap on her back door. "Glad to see you." She stepped aside as she opened the door. "But this must mean we're not having lunch."

Kristan handed her the letter of recommendation.

Tina quickly scanned it. "This is wonderful. Thank you. You really can write. I would hire me with this kind of recommendation." Tina frowned at her dog. "Go lay down."

Kristan replied, "Every word is the truth, and I was happy to do it."

Sparky continued to jump at Kristan's legs. "Go lay down," Tina said quietly. The dog went to her bed near the stove. "So what's going on today?"

"Got to be in court. It's really unexpected." Kristan turned back toward the door.

"Oh no, you don't. It's been weeks. You can spare a minute to talk to me while I get the kids up."

Kristan looked at her watch. "I have a few minutes."

"Anything special going on in court?"

"Just regular stuff, motions on some criminal cases I've been tracking."

"Anything important?"

"Not really, just time-consuming." Kristan followed Tina down the hall to Ashley's room. As the volunteer babysitter, she had been in this part of the house often. She leaned against the doorjamb and watched as Tina smiled down on the tousled-headed blond who was sound asleep under the down comforter.

"Hey, sleepyhead, time to get up for school," Tina said quietly.

Ashley popped up, all smiles as he rubbed his eyes to wipe away the gritty sleep. "Mom, I was dreaming." He stopped when he saw Kristan. He reached out his arms to give her a hug. "Hi, Kristan."

"Good morning, sweetpea." Kristan kissed him on the top of his head. She marveled at this ball of sunshine, who at age five loved to get up and go to kindergarten. How unlike Tina's nine-year-old twins, Dusty and Kelsey, who grumbled and groaned as they tried to sneak a couple of extra winks.

As if reading Kristan's thoughts, Tina nodded toward the bathroom door. "Dusty."

Kristan could hear Dusty in the bathroom, the short splash as water was turned on and off in the sink. She grinned at Tina.

"I want to hear a toothbrush going over some teeth," Tina yelled to her son. "I don't want to hear just the sound of water running."

"I know," Dusty whined.

"Mom, I have to have show and tell today," Kelsey said as she walked down the hallway pulling a sweatshirt over her head. "Oh. Hi, Kristan."

"Good morning, sunshine." Kristan wondered at Tina's calm in the face of such chaos. She thought about her own morning and the quiet she embraced each day.

"Kelsey, why didn't you tell me about this last night?" Tina sighed, the weight of motherhood suddenly heavy.

"I forgot," the nine-year-old said. "No big deal. Mrs. Hendricks doesn't care what it is," she said, heading for the kitchen.

"It is a big deal," Tina called after her. "Because it's your responsibility." She turned and looked at Kristan. "Any ideas?"

Kristan grinned. "Sorry, this is one area where I absolutely lack experience."

"Some mornings I wish I did too. But just some mornings."

"Mom, what's a show and something?" Ashley asked as he pulled half a dozen shirts from his dresser.

"Whoa, young man, pull out one shirt, not a handful, and put the rest back," Tina said distractedly as she refolded the clothes and returned them to the dresser. "Show and tell is when you take something to school and tell your class about it. Listen, pumpkin, you are old enough to know that you take out one shirt and leave the rest, okay?"

Ashley proudly held up the dark blue Winnie the Pooh shirt. "But I wanted to wear this one today." He smiled at Kristan.

"Mom, I need help with my math," Dusty said, exiting the bathroom. He looked up, saw Kristan and ignored her.

"Say hi," Tina ordered, her hands on her hips.

"Hi," he grumbled.

"Good morning," Kristan answered.

Tina shook her head. "Nine-year-olds. I can't wait until he's thirty."

"No, you don't. That will come soon enough." Kristan laughed.

"You said you didn't have any homework last night," Tina said wearily to her son.

"I forgot." He headed for his room. "Where's Dad?" Kristan knew he was attempting to circumvent his mother's further scrutiny, learning to avoid conflict just like his father.

"He already left for work." Tina surveyed the destruction to the bathroom. Wet towels dumped on the floor. The cap off the toothpaste. Toothpaste running down the side of the sink. She began gathering towels and shoving them into the hamper. She grabbed the scrub rag and wiped around the inside of the basin. Kristan watched her from the doorway.

"Mom, do I have to go to school?" Dusty called from the hallway.

"Yes," she answered evenly.

"Can't I just be sick today? Then I'll do my math and go tomorrow," he sulked.

"Absolutely not."

"Ah, Mom," he protested.

"Tell you what, I have a few minutes," Kristan said to Dusty. "I'm no math whiz, but I'll help you. Give your mother a breather."

"This is all shit," Dusty grumbled.

"What did you say?" Tina stepped into the hallway and watched his retreating back.

"Nothing," he yelled.

Tina sat down on the edge on the bathtub. She pushed her long blond hair off her neck. She clearly needed a moment before she joined the chaos in the kitchen. Tina knew that Ashley would have cereal spilled all over the table; Dusty and Kelsey would be arguing.

"A job will seem so much easier," she said quietly to Kristan.

"Are you so sure?"

"No question about it." Tina laughed.

Kristan wondered if Tina had told Billy about her plans for a job. She knew they were having problems; Tina had complained to her that he was coming in late at night with the smell of alcohol on his breath. Kristan knew Billy had promised, now that the kids were older, that he would spend more time at home.

There had been a respite from the nights out, a two-year gap after he traded a motorcycle he had rebuilt for a battered Nash. Kristan recalled how excited he had been the day the Nash pulled into their dooryard on the back of a wrecker. She had watched his restoration efforts. The pile of junk had become a car of beauty. It was gray with chrome trim, and he'd nicknamed it The Shadow.

Kristan had hoped it would be the ego boost Billy needed, but once the car was done, Tina had complained that the restlessness had returned. Ostensibly it was to show off the car, but lately it was just time away. Kristan had seen him at a bar she frequented. It wasn't that he was doing anything wrong, he was just hanging out, but she knew how much it bothered Tina.

"I'll go help Dusty. You catch your breath." Kristan hugged her friend.

"Thanks." Tina looked at the face in the mirror as she wiped out the sink, then looked at Kristan. "The homecoming queen, now the laundry queen." Her laugh lines had been replaced by stress lines.

"But a truly great laundry queen." Kristan reached over and pushed a strand of hair off of Tina's face.

"Mom, what should I use for show and tell?" Kelsey yelled from the kitchen.

"Better yet, I'll go help everyone out in the kitchen." Kristan patted her long-time friend on the shoulder.

A few minutes later, Tina appeared in the kitchen carrying a stuffed turtle, its head stretched as though reaching for an unseen fly. Kristan was bent over the math book helping Dusty.

"Here." Tina handed the turtle to her daughter. "Aunt Donna brought this back from Mexico last year. She got it at an open market in Mexico City. She said there were all kinds of animals that had been stuffed. Possums, raccoons, you name it. You know where Mexico is so you can talk about that and about her trip last year. Call her as soon as you eat your cereal. Okay?"

"Cool."

Within seconds, Tina had restored order. Kelsey was buttering some toast, and Ashley was spilling milk onto his cereal and onto the surrounding table.

Dusty stared at the open book in front of him. "I don't like math."

"I hated it. But ya gotta have it." Kristan rubbed her hand through his hair. He so reminded her of Billy.

"I don't like school."

"Too bad. You might as well get to like it, young man, because you have a bunch of years ahead of you," Tina said absently as she placed the turtle in Kelsey's knapsack.

Kelsey returned from phoning her aunt. "Aunt Donna said she hiked and camped all over Mexico. It's cool, Mom. I'll tell the kids at school."

Kristan glanced up at the clock. "Gotta go," she said to Tina. "Just a half page more and you'll be done," she told Dusty.

"Thanks, Kristan." Dusty grinned at her.

"You're welcome, tiger."

"See ya, pal." She gave Tina a hug and kissed Ashley on the head. "Knock 'em dead at show and tell," she told Kelsey. Kristan opened the door and picked up the newspaper. "Here, this is where the real chaos exists." She smiled at her friend. "I'll call you later. We'll set up a time to have lunch."

"You bet."

Kristan started the car. She and Tina had been friends when they were neighborhood kids, and as adults they reconnected when Kristan returned after college. Tina always complained that Kristan was having more fun chasing news stories than Tina was chasing dirty laundry.

Kristan thought about how different her friend's life might have been if she hadn't gotten pregnant with the twins. Kristan encouraged her to take some night classes at the college, and she finally acquiesced, but Kristan also knew that the night class had caused problems between Tina and Billy because it forced him to spend a night at home.

Chapter 4

After she left Tippys, Jennifer visited her office and talked with her secretary, Brenda. She had moved her file boxes in the week before. Today she would ignore the mess. As she left the office, she saw Kristan running into the courthouse. The two waved to each other, and Jennifer got into her Saab and headed home. She felt a rush. She had lived in apartments most of her adult life, and she could hardly believe that she now lived somewhere where the only person to slam a door would be her.

Thirty minutes later she drove slowly into her dooryard. She smiled at how quickly she had picked up that colloquial expression. It was her dooryard, not her driveway.

She could feel the stillness envelop her. A peace she had never found in the city surrounded her like a protective silk shield. Bailey's Cove, with its white church steeples, was across the bay. Every day at noon the carillon at the Congregational Church played. She stopped to listen. The name of the hymn escaped her but not the tranquillity it evoked. "I can get used to this," she told the large maple trees in her yard.

When she told her friends she was leaving Portland for Down East, they reacted with everything from shock to disappointment. Her friend Jeremy Cross, a fellow attorney in the D.A.'s office, told her that he couldn't live anyplace where he couldn't hear the world— the sound of traffic, the airplanes leaving Portland International. She missed him.

When she learned that she had inherited her grandmother's home, she knew her future was sealed. The move would be simple. She had no real ties in Portland, only friends. There had been a relationship, but, but, but. She was still relieved that the five-year relationship had ended. She had no frame of reference for the cheating, the endless lies, the lost nights when she worried where her ex was. But Pam had started calling soon after she arrived in Bailey's Cove. First there was the apology, then the talk of reconciliation. Jennifer continued to hold her at arm's length. "That's the past," she said as she hung her mental musings on the bush near the door and went inside.

The 150-year-old Cape still had its original woodwork. The woodwork would stay, but she was eager to begin stripping the walls of the dark flowery wallpaper and replacing it with muted paint tones.

She climbed the stairs to the second-floor bedrooms. She had picked the largest one for her bedroom, but it would be only a matter of months before she knocked down the adjoining wall to create a roomy master bedroom. She slipped out of her skirt and hung it neatly on a hanger. She tossed her blouse into the hamper and pulled off the black half-slip, dark pantyhose and red lace bra then dove into her running suit.

Downstairs, she poured herself a glass of this year's first batch of sun tea, then sat at the antique circular oak kitchen table, its ice cream chairs circled around it like wagons around a campfire. She liked working for Francis. She respected his mind and the way he combined rough humor with an almost courtly demeanor. He had practiced law Down East for forty years, and he still cared about people. She hated the thought of her trip to Portland and the move. She wished a genie would appear and take care of that part of her life. She had planned to be away at least two weeks, but she'd made up her mind to expedite that. She longed for the solitude of the area.

She thought about Kristan. In Portland, Jennifer had avoided reporters. Even in the few high-profile cases she had been involved with, she left the press dogs to the bosses. They wanted one thing only, the unfortunate slip or sensational comment that would be the banner headline in the morning paper. But she knew she would have to deal with Kristan and Toby. Francis said that Kristan—the more aggressive reporter of the two—could be trusted. He also had made it clear that he would not be around to handle a lot of the cases. She sipped her sun tea and wondered if Kristan and Toby were lovers.

Chapter 5

Kristan raced through the familiar courthouse and up the black oak staircase that circled its way to superior court on the second floor. The large solid wooden doors stood as a barrier between her and the proceedings inside. She stopped to collect her breath. She had quit smoking years ago, but she still got winded during a fast climb up some stairs.

The doors were closed so she knew the judge was already on the bench. She put both hands against the door and eased it open. Shit, she thought. She had left Tina's house early enough to be on time. This was not her case. She had sprinted for no reason.

The judge was listening intently to attorney Bill Case. A young man in a dark suit sat next to him. Kristan quickly processed the scene. This had to be a divorce. Attorney Fred Hartman was on the other side of the courtroom, a woman seated next to him.

Kristan hesitated. She could go back downstairs and trade insults with the court clerks, or sit and wait. She looked up at the antique clock, its large silver pendulum swinging back and forth. Motions for the criminal cases had been set for ten a.m. It was just a little after that. Judge Timothy Alexander ran a strict courtroom; attorneys did not lag.

Except for entering a few notes into a laptop computer on his desk, the judge looked bored as he listened to the attorneys detail the division of assets. When Case paused to look down at his notes, Alexander asked, "Is that it?"

"Yes, Your Honor."

"Anything from you, counselor?" He looked at the other attorney.

"No, Your Honor." Fred Hartman answered. "Those are the conditions our clients agreed upon."

"I find that there are irreconcilable differences and the divorce is granted." Alexander rose. "Court is in recess for fifteen minutes."

"All rise," bailiff Jim Blake ordered.

Kristan felt the tension dip with the departure of the judge. Although the attorneys were shaking hands in that respectful good-old-boy style, neither the woman nor the man would look at each other. Hartman walked back to his client and whispered something to her. She nodded and rose. With her head held perfectly straight, she walked past the table where her ex-husband sat.

Kristan wondered what the woman was thinking. Simple solutions, she thought. No need for a doctor here; a judge had sliced their lives in half.

The husband conferred with his attorney and then, after a respectful period to give his ex-wife time to get out of the courthouse, he got up and left.

"What are you doing here?" Case asked Kristan as he stuffed papers into his briefcase.

"You're not chasing kiss-and-split cases, are you?" Fred called to her.

"Please, gentlemen, news does not stoop that low." Kristan feigned insult. "Naw, I'm waiting for action on some motions on some cases I've been tracking."

"Anything interesting?" Case asked.

"Motion to suppress an alleged arsonist's confession. You remember the fire last year, the guy got mad and burned down his girlfriend's house."

"Yeah, I remember. Well, keep them honest." Case turned to Hartman. "Got time for coffee?"

"Sure."

"Hey, how ya doing?" Kristan greeted Toby. "I didn't think you'd be here to cover this."

Toby nodded to the two attorneys who were leaving. "Had to talk to you. Boy, it's been busy since breakfast. I was going to call you, but when I got back to the station I had to sit in for one of the deejays. He went home sick."

"How about a drink tonight?"

"Can't. Got to fill in again tonight. Jeff's still out sick. Got this flu thing. I wasn't going to cover this, but I thought you might be here. It's been hours since we talked. Where've you been? What you been doing? Have you been over to Francis's office?"

Kristan loved his rapid-fire questions. It was a game they played to see how many questions could be remembered and answered. "Let's see. I've been here or at Tina's. I've been up to my neck in news. And no."

"Very good. All I can say is wow, not to your answers, but to the new prosecutor."

Kristan laughed. "That's all you can say?"

"I've got to go out with that woman. I've been thinking about her since we all had breakfast this morning."

"Well, go out with her then. She's said she'll be back in a few weeks."

"I know. Isn't she just everything you've ever dreamed up?"

Kristan cocked her eyebrow at Toby. "Well, not everything."

Toby laughed. "Well," he said, "just about everything."

"Ask her out."

He leaned over to Kristan. "Why don't we both ask her out and see which of us wins?"

Kristan socked him hard in the arm. He leaned back in his chair and laughed.

Suddenly the court clerk and court reporter were back. Kristan looked around. The courtroom had filled up with several people waiting for their cases to be called. The loud rap on the door brought her back to the reason she was there, and she and everyone else rose to their feet.

"All rise, the Honorable Judge Timothy Alexander presiding," the court bailiff intoned.

Kristan listened to the attorneys as they argued their client's position. She was bored. Toby's reference to Jennifer had distracted her from the cases at hand. She wondered if the woman was gay.

Later that day, Kristan stared at the cursor blinking rhythmically on her screen. It reminded her of the unremitting blip on a heart monitor, only no one would die if this one stopped.

She edited her story again. The attorney had made a case for why the judge should grant his motion to suppress his client's confession, but the state's Attorney General had been just as convincing as to why the judge shouldn't. The judge said he would rule on the motion in a few days. She pushed the alt-print screen buttons to check the spelling. After that it would fly from Bailey's Cove to Bangor in a nanosecond.

The telephone interrupted her halfway through the check process. She glanced at the caller ID and smiled. "Hey, pal."

"You and that damn caller ID," her friend Jackie Claymont said.

"I like it. At first I thought it was just another electronic nuisance, but it's great for screening calls."

"Well, I liked it better when I at least got in the first word. You free tonight?"

"What did you have in mind?"

"Supper, my house, say around seven-thirty."

"Cool. What can I bring?"

"Just you."

"See you soon." Kristan leaned back in her chair. It was six-thirty. She would have just enough time to freshen up, then head over to Jackie's.

Jackie was her oldest friend. They had been next-door friends growing up. Even though Jackie was a few years older, Kristan had been absolutely infatuated with her, and she used to follow her all over the neighborhood. When Jackie got her first twowheel bike, Kristan begged her father for one. She was six years old and it was the first time she took a stand against her father, unsure of how he would react. She even refused to ride her tricycle; it was too childish next to Jackie's two-wheeler. Her father's mood was right, and there was no temper tantrum or fight, no need to brace for the familiar punch, just a used two-wheeler on the back porch one morning.

Jackie taught her to ride. Kristan recalled the first time she let go of the handlebars, confident in her abilities. They wobbled and then swung sharply toward her, connecting with her crotch. She and the bike tumbled onto the cement. It would be years before she let go of the handlebars again.

The two friends had been apart many times, first when Jackie left for college and later when she went to medical school. But after a couple of years residency at Massachusetts General Hospital, Jackie returned home to start a medical practice. She also on occasion— when someone died violently or unexpectedly—served as the Bailey Cove's medical examiner.

Even when they were separated, they never lost the closeness of their friendship.

Three years ago, on Jackie's first day back in town, Kristan stood at her door with three squirmy lobsters while Jackie introduced her friend Marianne. They reconnected immediately.

She punched the keys to send her copy to Bangor and watched the bounceback on her screen. She dialed the toll-free number and waited for Jerry to answer. Sometimes letters and words were trapped forever in the ancient telephone lines that connected the city with the county. If it was raining, the problem was exacerbated and assignment editors might get a story that was garbled or missing two or three lines.

"Where will you be if I have a question?" Jerry asked after confirming delivery of the story.

"Out, but just leave a message on my answering machine, and I'll check it around eight."

"Good." Jerry was gone.

"Hey, you," Jackie said. The orange and yellow flames from the giant fireplace that dominated her living room reflected in her glasses. "Are you here or somewhere else?" They had been staring at the fire, comfortable in their silence.

"Somewhere else for a minute."

"Bad day?"

"Not really. Just went to see my father." Kristan knew she did not have to explain the depression she felt after visiting her father in the nursing home. "Jacks, have you ever felt that moments from your childhood define who you are?"

"Where are you going with this?"

"Bad relationships."

"Thinking of anyone in particular?"

"I've been thinking a lot about Patti. How I fooled around on her. I deserve this celibate punishment."

"Why are you thinking about it now?"

"Don't know. Well, I think I do. I met the new A.D.A. today."

"Ah. Do you regret what you did?"

"Absolutely." Kristan sipped at her wine.

"You want to talk about it."

"We've talked it to death in the past. It's just my blue period. But enough of this maudlin crap, how was your day?"

"It was okay, quiet at the clinic. It's April—sniffles, colds, a lot of bronchitis. Margie is leaving."

"Your lab tech? Where?"

"Marrying a fella from Bangor. Want a job?"

"Yeah, right. I'd be great at it. I'd throw up at the sight of blood and faint if someone vomited."

"I think it's the other way around, my friend."

"See, that's why you wouldn't want me."

"Heard all about the new A.D.A." Jackie returned to the barb that was pricking Kristan.

"Uhmm."

"Is she?"

"Don't know. I think probably not."

"Cute?"

"Cute." Kristan made a curt, dismissive motion. "I find that one-word question curious."

Jackie grinned. "The word is in vogue. I hear it at the clinic all day long. I understand you had breakfast with her."

Kristan sighed in resignation. "The talking drums. Faster than anything I can get in the paper. She and Francis were at Tips."

"So what's she like?"

"Young, bright, articulate; young."

"How young?"

"Thirty, maybe thirty-one. Francis was high on her. Enthusiastic. She seemed comfortable with him. She'll probably be good."

"What's she look like?"

"I don't know, Jacks. Her eyes, nose and mouth were all in the right places." Kristan paused. "Attractive, not pretty, certainly not 'cute,'" she added with disdain for the word.

"And was everything else in the right place?" Jackie teased.

Kristan groaned.

Jackie poured herself a glass of the chilled wine and topped off Kristan's. "You like her?"

"Yeah, probably. I think she'll be okay to work with. Truth be told, it's too early to tell. The test comes when I'm on deadline and I need a comment, or she loses a case and doesn't want to talk."

"You attracted to her?"

Kristan shrugged. "I am always in pursuit of Eros."

"You're horny."

"Jeez, I wouldn't pigeonhole it as that. I like the chase. The romance." The long pregnant pause. "I am attracted to her, but so is Toby."

"Uh-oh."

"No, not uh-oh. He's a cool guy, a good friend. If she's straight he'd be a good guy for her."

"And if she's not, or if she's curious?"

"I don't know. I'm not really into curious." Kristan sipped her wine. She felt at peace for the first time in weeks. "I'm not sure I want to complicate things in my life right now."

"Invite her to go beachcombing."

"Just like that? I just call her up and say 'Want to go beachcombing?'"

"It's that simple."

"Sounds too much like a date."

"Yikes, you have been out of circulation too long. Dinner is a date. Beachcombing is something you do with friends. Lovers too, but also friends."

"I don't know."

"I am talking friendship, my little buddy. Not marriage. Ask her to go beachcombing."

"I'll think about it."

Jackie clearly sensed her resistance. "Kris, what's wrong?"

"You have a crystal ball under that T-shirt?"

Jackie patted her stomach. "No, just me. But I know you and—"

"And, and, and," Kristan repeated like a mantra. "I think I'm losing me." She slipped backward again into her morass, then added, "Not physically." She noted the concern in Jackie's eyes. "My spirit is gone, Jacks, the passion for the chase. Not for love, for news." Kristan rubbed her index finger against her lips. "I don't think a news story exists anymore that I can feel passionate about."

"Do something else."

"I can't."

"Just like that?"

"They pay too good. I've sold my soul for a byte, that's spelled b-y-t-e." Kristan laughed.

Jackie grinned. "You can't be losing it too badly. Come on, let's finish this conversation over beans and wieners." Kristan followed her friend into her large kitchen. Brown juice bubbled down the side of the crock pot. Jackie popped four wieners into the microwave. "Grab a plate. You know where the silverware is. Here." She handed Kristan a soup ladle and at the same moment lifted the glass top from the beans.

"Gee, that smells good." Kristan inhaled. She ladled two spoonfuls onto her plate. The microwave dinged and Jackie dumped two wieners in the middle of Kristan's beans. Kristan reached for the ketchup and onions.

Jackie had her head buried in the refrigerator. "Milk, Coke, juice?"

"Milk." Kristan pulled out a chair and put her plate down.

Jackie set her plate piled high with soupy beans across from Kristan's. "Really, why not quit?"

"I don't know what I would do."

"You're a good writer. So write. Write a book, or a magazine article. Freelance. Wash dishes."

"I could write romance novels." Kristan smirked. "'Clara loves Ceil.' One thing I have learned though. If I wrote one, there would be a lot of chase. Lesbians like the romantic chase. The electricity between two women. Women like romance."

"Ahhh, I doubt you've had enough experience for that."

"What? Writing or romance?" Kristan feigned irritation. "I've had enough experience in both."

"Right, Miss 'I am always going to be celibate.'"

Kristan shrugged. "How would folks here take to a gay novelist?"

"Like they take to everything else. You're one of their own. They'd gossip behind your back of course, but no one would throw stones at your house."

"Did you have problems when you and Marianne first moved back?"

"Not really. Everybody loved her. Funny, we were a couple, but around here we were just 'the girls.'" There was a long pause. Marianne had died of cancer two years before. Jackie—the person, not the doctor—rarely spoke of that moment. Jackie the lover never talked about the loss.

"Jacks, I miss her too," Kristan said softly.

"You know, it's been two years, yet when I'm alone, I find myself talking to her. Now, that's losing it."

"No. She was special."

Jackie shrugged off the melancholy. "Getting back to you and your psyche, my young friend."

"Not so young anymore." Kristan smiled.

"Do something, babe. I've watched you this past year and you are not happy in either your professional or personal life. Right now you feel trapped. The job pays well, I grant you. You're forty-plus, so making changes becomes a greater challenge. And security is a hell of lot better than insecurity. But you can't go on with this depression. You brood. You're moody."

"Is it really that bad?"

"Yeah, it's really that bad."

"But I don't know what I want. I like parts of my life. It's just some parts I don't like."

"Shit." Jackie pulled the beeper off her belt and studied the number. "It's the clinic." She grabbed for what Kristan called her pretend-a-phone, the cordless receiver that sat always within an arm's reach. "Let's hope it's only a minor emergency."

Chapter 6

Kristan pushed her cart around the Shop 'n Save. It had been ages since she had been in the store at six on a work night. Usually news took longer than that. She was staring at the asparagus and trying to decide if she could afford $3.99 a pound.

"You're an asparagus woman."

Kristan jumped. "You're back!" She realized she was pleased. She would have recognized that voice anywhere. It was deep, sexy and as warm and inviting as hot cocoa on a cold winter morning.

"Yup, got back Monday. Been in court all day." Jennifer was smiling at her. Her mahogany eyes danced with intrigue.

"Well, glad you're back."

"Thank you." Jennifer smiled mischievously.

"Good day in court?" Kristan felt uncomfortable with the too-flirtatious tone they were using.

"Not bad. Francis seemed pleased. A bunch of plea bargains, and we got some of those who wanted continuances to enter pleas."

"Good." Kristan shifted from foot to foot. "You want to have coffee, or something?"

"Yeah. Is it okay to be seen with you?"

"I don't bite."

"I mean, is it okay for you and me to be seen together? We are on opposite sides."

Kristan ran her hand through her hair. "Aw, this is Jefferson County. I have coffee with everyone."

"Everyone." Jennifer arched an eyebrow. "Okay, you're on for a cup of coffee. Where?"

"McDonald's in about—" Kristan looked at her watch. "Thirty minutes?"

"See you there." Jennifer pushed her cart past the vegetables and down the next aisle.

Kristan picked one of the back booths at McDonald's. She greeted several people she knew when she walked in, but she wore her "I don't wish to be bothered" look, hoping that no one would come up to her with what they felt was a smashing news story that, as was usually the case, would turn out to be a bust. She had rushed through her food-shopping so she wouldn't keep Jennifer waiting. That was a first. Kristan kept most people, including the mayor, waiting.

Jennifer entered and looked around at the group of fried-food junkies then spotted Kristan.

Cute? Kristan wondered. Why did people keep calling her *cute?* Nice-looking, not pretty. Full-framed, not slender. Attractive face, with eyes that invited confidence. But definitely not cute.

She noticed that Jennifer had switched from the lavender suit she had on at the food store to jeans and a tight white Danskin top. She had on a lush black-suede bomber jacket.

"Hi," she said as she slid into the booth. "Have you ordered?"

"No, but let me get whatever you'd like."

"Are you having coffee?"

"No, I never touch it, but I'll get you a cup. Want a hamburger? Something else?"

"Thanks, just coffee, with two creams."

Kristan made her way across the restaurant. This time it was unavoidable. Several people stopped to speak with her. They were curious about the woman she was with.

Jennifer smiled to herself as she watched Kristan. Did she ever dress up? she wondered. Since her return, she had watched from her office window as Kristan went into the courthouse. Her wardrobe was consistent—blue jeans with a button-down fly, blouse, T-shirt and a light blue-denim jacket, collar turned up. The only things that changed day-to-day were the T-shirt or sweatshirt, sometimes pink or red, green or blue. Jennifer also noted that Kristan's socks matched her top. And she had on white running shoes that really were white.

Although the clothes lacked imagination, there was something charmingly feminine about her. She liked her short blond hair and the windblown look that Jennifer suspected was the result of pushing her hands through her hair rather than of the wind.

"Do you ever dress up?" she asked as Kristan set a steaming hot cup of coffee in front of her. Great, she thought. She'll think I'm criticizing her clothes. Jennifer bit her lip.

Kristan stared down at her clothes. "Oh, yeah." She grinned good-naturedly as she sipped a Coke. "Every now and then I buy a new sweatshirt at Ames or Wal-Mart. That's pretty dressy by Down East standards. Although I have to admit there have been times when I've had to really dress up." She paused for effect. "At weddings and funerals. Then I usually swap the sweatshirt for a vest."

Jennifer laughed.

"We're pretty casual about clothes down here. The rest of the world is worrying about what to wear. Not here. Look around you."

Kristan's gesture included all of the restaurant. "Men in jeans, women in jeans or slacks." Kristan shifted under Jennifer's stare and she blinked. Jennifer knew that her stare had caused many a suspect to squirm in a courtroom seat. "You getting ready to cross-examine me?" Kristan teased.

"I'm sorry, I didn't mean to stare." Jennifer felt her nerves humming like a power line. "I am curious about who you are."

"Born here, went to elementary and high school here. Left immediately after graduation, went to the University of Maine. Studied journalism. Came back here and started working at a weekly. Now I'm with a daily. End of story. What about you?"

"Born in Portland, went to school there. Attended the University of Southern Maine, then law school. Graduated. Worked in the D.A.'s office in Portland, finally transferred up here."

"Ah," Kristan exhaled. "Just as fascinating. Are you usually this entertaining?"

"No, actually, I tend to be quite boring."

"I doubt that." Kristan sipped her Coke. Jennifer flushed. "Have you family?"

"My father and mother live in Portland. They're teachers. My dad teaches high-school mathematics. His greatest pain in life was that as far as math was concerned, I just didn't get it. Mom's a music teacher. I'm an only child, although if you ask my parents, they'll tell you they did not spoil me. I'm not sure I agree with them. And as you know, my grandmother recently passed away, leaving me her house."

"Lucky us," Kristan said impulsively.

Jennifer frowned, uncertain about this woman's humor.

"I'm not being sarcastic. I'm serious. Lucky us. Francis is getting on in years, and—" Kristan studied the plastic cup that held her Coke. "He's slipping a bit. But even now at his age he's got more law in his head than most law school graduates."

"Agreed," Jennifer said. "But you know—" She cradled her warm cup of coffee. "He's seventy-seven and he's entitled to slip a little. But I plan to be there to cover those slips. I know I can do that for him."

"I like that and so will a lot of other people. He is much loved. Can you imagine being a county prosecutor for more than forty years and even the bad guys don't hold a grudge?"

"I hope I can be half that successful."

"I suspect you will be, if you stay." Kristan held up her hand to stop the protest. "Wait, wait, let me tell you about my two-year rule."

"I can't wait."

"Well, I've found that among people who weren't born and raised here, those . . ." She placed her hand against her chest as if to emphasize the seriousness of her words. "Those people who come from away and stay more than two years" Kristan sipped her Coke—"there is a ninety-five percent chance they will continue to live here. But if they are going to leave, it will more than likely be within the first two years. So, for you the clock is ticking."

"You're making that up."

"No, no, I have unimpeachable proof."

"What's your bet, will I break your two-year rule?"

"I can't predict. In fact, I have found that I am the world's worst predictor, even though I invented the two-year premise. Sixteen months ago, the Jefferson County Technical College hired a woman academic vice president. She left several weeks ago to finish her doctorate. She and I used to go out to dinner on occasion. It is lonely here for people who don't have family." Kristan stopped. "And then there was a priest I got to know. He was here less than two years too."

"Did you and the priest have dinner?"

"Yes, at least once a month."

"Well maybe that's the problem. Maybe people would stay longer if they didn't go out to dinner with you."

Kristan's smile was provocative. "Actually, I've thought about that. Maybe that is the single denominator. Hmm, I guess I won't ask you to go to dinner. How about beachcombing?"

"But maybe it's not a good idea anyway." Jennifer bit her tongue. "I mean, I'd like to go beachcombing with you sometime. But that might be a problem."

"How so?"

"Jobs, Kristan. Reporter-prosecutor. Remember? You're here to make my life living hell."

"Nah, that's not how it is here. Some of my best friends are cops and attorneys. This is not New York or L.A. We write about cases won and lost, but an exposé about the D.A.'s office? That's bull. There never ever has been a hint of scandal about the D.A.'s office. No murder, mayhem or sex."

"None?"

"Nada. My rules are simple." Kristan paused. "If I'm in pursuit of a story, and I need information, just tell it to me straight. If it's off the record, tell me. Don't lie. Don't stonewall. Just tell me. I maintain confidentiality, and I take everyone on faith."

"Ever been burned?"

"In my professional life? Never."

"And in your personal life?"

"No comment, counselor."

"Well, I learned something about handling the press when I was in Portland."

"What was that?"

"Volunteer nothing, deny everything and demand proof."

Kristan raised her Coke in acknowledgment. "We're going to do just fine, counselor, just fine. Now how about it? Would you like to go beachcombing? I have to work the next two weekends, but the weekend after that might be good."

"You're on, Ms. Newshound."

Kristan exhaled. She didn't realize that she had been holding her breath. Jackie would be pleased.

Chapter 7

Jennifer frowned at the documents in front of her. Her mind kept wandering back to Kristan. They had run into each other almost every day since she came back. And although the visits were short, there was a flirtatious edge to their conversations. She realized she was looking forward to their beachcombing date and wished it was this weekend instead of the next one. She could hear the *tap-tap* of her secretary's computer through her closed door. She had given Brenda several reports to type that she needed for district court on Monday.

Brenda stared at the copy. She was having trouble deciphering Jennifer's handwriting but was reluctant to interrupt her because Jennifer had asked her not to unless there was a national emergency. She had been working for her for only a few weeks, but she already felt a fierce loyalty to her. She suspected Jennifer brought that emotion out in everyone. The secretary puzzled over two words that were difficult to read and did not look up as the door opened. "What the heck is this?" she mumbled to herself.

"Hi, is Jennifer Ogden in?" the woman asked.

"Yes, but she can't be disturbed. Can I help you?"

"Just ring through on your little telephone there and tell her Portland attorney Pam Rivers is here. She'll interrupt for me."

As the woman put both hands on Brenda's desk and leaned over authoritatively, Brenda frowned. She was unimpressed with her cat-green eyes, the fingerdeep dimples in each cheek and her pushy manner.

She knew the woman was not from around Jefferson County; her expensive cashmere jacket and tight-fitting designer jeans did not suit the Jefferson County look. Three gold chains with various lockets hung from her neck. A two-stone diamond ring fit her left pinkie finger. For Brenda, it was instant dislike.

"I'm sorry, she asked not to be disturbed. She is preparing for a case, and I just won't do it." Brenda was digging in, ready to do battle with this woman.

Pam leaned even farther across the desk and smiled, but Brenda could see the smile had not spread to her eyes. "I will take responsibility for the interruption. Either you announce me or I look behind each and every door. I didn't drive six hours from Portland to be turned away by a secretary."

Brenda stood up and glanced protectively at Jennifer's door. "Well, this is one secretary who is not going to do your bidding. You might get away with that down there in Portland, but secretaries here in Bailey's Cove"—Brenda's voice flared with contempt—"are not intimidated by your 'from-away' ways."

"Quaint, 'from-away ways,' " Pam mimicked. "You don't need to announce me. I saw you look at that door, and I bet Jennifer is behind it." She turned, walked toward Jennifer's office and opened the door before Brenda could protest.

"Brenda, I said—" Jennifer stopped as Pam entered the room.

"Hi," Pam said softly as she closed the door behind her.

"I bet you didn't make friends with my new secretary if you got in here." The soft knock on her door stopped her. "Come in."

"I'm sorry, Jennifer, but—" Brenda glared at the intruder, and Pam smiled confidently back at her.

"It's okay, Brenda." Jennifer looked from Brenda to Pam. "I'll handle this. Has Francis left?"

"Yes."

"If you go to lunch, just lock the outside door. I'll take care of this." She waited as Brenda softly closed the door. "I expected you to arrive at my door someday. I figured the telephone conversations wouldn't be enough."

"Pretty confident, huh." Pam perched on the edge of Jennifer's desk.

Jennifer could smell her perfume, Red, and although in the past the smell had melted her at the most difficult moments, she now found it slightly disturbing, and not in a romantic way.

"I've missed you," Pam said softly. "And you're right, the telephone wasn't enough."

Jennifer stared at her.

"You're not going to make this easy?"

"This isn't going to work. Your being here puts too much pressure on me." Jennifer ran her hands through her hair in frustration.

"I want to see you when we talk. I want to hold you. To make love to you."

"For now, it's going to be just talk." Jennifer kept the desk between her and Pam.

"Well, I was thinking about something a little less formal. Look, I'm here for the weekend. I think we need to give us a chance."

Jennifer stood up and went from her desk to her window. "There is no *us*. After your involvement with 'the other woman,' I found myself thinking in terms of being single—you know, one egg for breakfast, a single cup of coffee. A single bed."

Pam walked up behind her, her breath caressing the back of Jennifer's neck. Jennifer shivered, remembering the nights they had lain spooning after making love, Pam's warm body against her back.

Pam said, "You can't forget five years. Look, I've changed. After you left I realized that you were the only good thing I had in my life. I knew I had blown it, and I am here to say I'm sorry, it will never happen again."

"You've promised that before."

"Yeah, but this is the first time you've left permanently. This move scared the shit out of me." Pam touched Jennifer's shoulder. "I love you. I now know I can never love anyone else."

Jennifer turned around and stared into Pam's eyes. Those bewitching eyes that dissolved into an even darker green when they were passionate. "Pam, I've never thought for a minute that you didn't love me. In fact, I know you love me. You just can't stop loving other women as well. At first I was angry, bitter, now I just feel a huge void."

"I want to fill that void," Pam said. Her hand grazed Jennifer's cheek. "I want to make it up to you."

Jennifer felt her resolve weakening, but then she stepped back against the window and rested against the sill. Pam closed the gap between them.

"Don't rush this, Pam. Also, this is not exactly the place where I even want to discuss a reconciliation." She pushed Pam away from her and out of her space.

Pam laughed, clearly buoyed, no doubt because Jennifer had used the word *reconciliation*. "All right. I forget this is the country, where it wouldn't do to have two women kissing in the D.A.'s office."

"No, it wouldn't do even if I wanted to. Look, I have a few more hours of work."

"How about lunch?"

"How about dinner. Why don't you meet me back here, say, at six?"

"I need a place to stay."

Jennifer sighed. "I expected you would."

"I want to stay with you. I came prepared to stay with you." Her voice took on an assertive tone.

Jennifer nodded in acknowledgment, not trusting her voice.

Pam walked to the door. "See you at six," she said gently, then closed the door behind her.

Jennifer sat staring at the clock. Her decision to work had been reduced to moving papers and pushing a pencil idly across the yellow legal pad in front of her. It was the pretense of work.

When she arrived in Cranberry Bluffs, she had secretly hoped Pam would show up on her doorstep, her green BMW trailing behind a large U-Haul truck that carried all her belongings. There would have been yet another reconciliation and the promise of new beginnings, but now Jennifer couldn't decide how she really felt.

When she got tired of thinking with a pencil, she began to pace. At five-thirty she turned off her computer, stacked her papers on her desk and walked out of her office.

Brenda had left a half-hour earlier. Jennifer walked over to Francis's office and looked inside. He was already gone for the weekend.

She looked out the window and saw the green BMW waiting in the parking lot. Jennifer pulled a jacket from the coat hook and met Pam as she stepped out of the car.

"Hi. I was afraid you might have run off."

"I gave it some serious thought." Jennifer laughed for the first time.

"I'm glad you didn't, and I am glad for the laugh. I've truly missed you." Pam reached up and touched Jennifer's cheek.

Jennifer flushed and looked around. "It is much more difficult being open here than in Portland, I guess."

"Most people will just think we're two old friends. It will mean nothing."

"Don't bet on it. You've never lived in a small town. Everything means something here."

Kristan turned around in her chair and looked out the window. Her impatience was rising as she spoke with her assignment editor. Then she saw Jennifer and watched as the woman with her reached out and touched her cheek. She dropped the telephone.

"Ah no, Jerry," she said to her editor as she scrambled to pick up the telephone. "I'm here. Sorry, I dropped the telephone."

"Well, anyway, I've got your story, so I'll talk to you later," he said.

Kristan replaced the receiver. She felt like a voyeur as she watched the women. She could sense their intimacy, the way the woman's fingers lingered on Jennifer's cheek. Kristan felt her spirits fall.

Well, so much for fantasy. She threw her reporter's notebook across the room. It caromed off the wall and landed on the floor. She walked over and quietly picked it up. This is too primal, she scolded herself.

She paced the small office. There had been no hints other than a few flirtatious moments when she and Jennifer had been at McDonald's. Frustrated, she shoved her hands in her pockets. She regretted listening to Jackie. Now she was stuck with going beach-combing with Jennifer next weekend. How to get out of it was all she could think about.

She sat back down at her computer, slammed her fingers against the keys and watched strange letters rush across the screen.

"Take control," she said aloud. She felt the panic rising in her chest. "Take control." She reached for her telephone and dialed the clinic. "Hi, it's Kristan. Is Jackie free?"

"Sorry, Kristan, she's at the hospital making rounds. I don't expect to see her back here today. She said something about going home after her rounds and catching up on an old movie," Jackie's receptionist, Betty Clark, said. "Give her an hour or so and you'll probably catch her there."

"Thanks, Betty."

Kristan turned back to her window. The parking lot was empty; Jennifer and the other woman were gone. She shut down her computer and left her office. She needed air.

"I want to do more than talk," Pam said as she inched closer to Jennifer on the couch. "I want to hold you."

Over dinner, Jennifer had been careful to keep their conversation away from their relationship and focused on mutual friends or cases they were working on. When they returned to Jennifer's house she had shown Pam to the guest room, and although there had been a questioning look, there was no pressure from her former lover.

"Pam, I can't. My emotions are just too raw. The feelings going on in me right now are so conflicting. There are moments when I want to melt in your arms and moments when I just want to sock you."

"I vote for the melting in my arms. Look, I love you. Ever since you left, I have not been with another woman. I don't want another woman. I don't want this to be too late."

Jennifer felt herself being drawn to Pam. She felt the pull of five years of intimacy, an intimacy she had never shared with anyone else.

The clock on the mantel chimed midnight and Jennifer frowned. "Let's talk again tomorrow. This has been a lot of emotion to process in a short period of time. We have two more days. If it happens," Jennifer said softly, "it happens."

"I want it to happen." Pam took Jennifer's hand and kissed her palm. "I won't push. Just know that I love you and I will always love you."

Chapter 8

Jennifer awoke early Saturday. She quietly got up, walked down to the kitchen and tried to push back the alarm that was growing inside her. Don't panic, she told herself. Just wait and see how this goes. She heard Pam's steps behind her.

Pam stood next to her, staring out the window at the bay. "This is beautiful, Jennifer. I can see why you gave up Portland—aside from your problems with me," Pam said quickly.

"Each day I thank my grandmother for giving me this. I thought at first I'd get used to looking at that bay, but I haven't. Every day is different. This place has more changing faces"—her hand swept outward to encompass the bay— "than any place I've ever lived. Sunrises are thrilling. I make it a point to be up. And there have been twilights when the full moon seems to rise up out of the water and you feel like you can reach out and touch it. This place has a spring face and now I am looking forward to its summer side." Jennifer stopped.

"I'm happy for you." Pam touched Jennifer's arm. Jennifer turned toward her and stepped into her embrace. It felt so familiar. "I've missed you," Pam said against her neck.

"It's strange. I find I've missed you." Jennifer was tentative. She stepped back. "Strange."

"Not so strange."

"I was so hurt when I found out. I felt like I was not going to be able to ever again put one foot in front of the other." She stared straight into Pam's eyes. She marveled at the woman's ability to stare back without even a hint of guilt. "Then the hurt left, and I found that I really didn't care if there was another woman. It was almost a relief, something like getting permission to go on with my life. Does that make sense?" Jennifer stepped over to the counter and the coffeemaker. "Because I somehow knew there would always be another woman."

"Yeah, strangely, it does make sense. Before I could never explain it, but now I think I am beginning to understand me. I've been seeing a woman." Pam held up her hands to stop Jennifer's expected reaction. "A psychologist, and we've been doing the whole head thing. I'm not certain I am a hundred percent through with whatever it is that keeps me chasing women like a dog in heat, but I do know that I began to examine our relationship at a depth I had never allowed myself to do before, and I found I needed you, in my life."

Jennifer held her breath.

Pam leaned over and kissed her cheek, breaking the tension. "I'm glad I'm here. You know what I would like to do today?"

"What?"

"I'd like to do the tourist thing. We never seemed to get here when your grandmother was alive, so I think it would be fun. Let's go beachcombing."

"You're on." Jennifer felt relief. With Pam's confessed statement of seeing a psychologist, she felt herself teetering on the edge.

"Jennifer, can I ask you a personal question?" They were standing on Jennifer's rocky beach, their shoulders touching as they watched the lobster boats bouncing on the waves.

"Sure."

"I didn't exactly expect you to fall in my arms when I arrived, but I sense something different in you." Pam turned toward her. "Have you met someone?"

Averting her gaze, Jennifer paused a long time before answering. "I'm not sure." She picked her way among the rocks. "I was just thinking about her. It's always been eerie the wavelength that you and I seem to be on. She's a reporter."

"Ouch."

"No, not like what we faced in Portland. She's good, trustworthy, ethical."

"An ethical reporter? Definitely an oxymoron. That is not the word I would use to describe a reporter. More like unprincipled, unscrupulous, disreputable, corrupted, treacherous."

"Okay, okay." Jennifer laughed. "I get the picture, but she's not like that."

Pam turned and stopped her with a hand on her arm. "Who is she?"

"Her name is Kristan Cassidy, and I'd say she's maybe twelve years older than me."

"Ah, you're in the mood for an older-model lover." Pam's tone was bitter.

"Come on Pam, you've slept with older, used and late-model lovers. Age never stopped you, not even when we were together." Jennifer felt the mindless frustration again. This was not where she wanted to go with her feelings.

"Yeah, and that was my downfall. Older used models, younger newer models." She stopped, as if sensing the shift. The words had hit a responsive chord. "I will fight for you. All those models are in

49

my past." Pam stepped toward her, her expression an image of hope and desire.

Jennifer turned and continued her walk along the beach. Pam was silent for a long time.

"It's none of my business, but have you slept with her?"

Jennifer sensed Pam's tight rein on her anger. "You're right, it's none of your business, but the answer is no, and I don't know that I will. I'm getting to know her, and I suspect if anyone initiates the move it will have to be me." She was surprised at the nakedness of her statement. She never had been the aggressor in a relationship, and this was the first time she had focused on who would have to make the first move.

"What is this some, kind of femme thing?"

"No."

"I have to admit, from a jealous perspective, I'm glad you haven't slept with her."

"I expected you would be."

"Just out of potent curiosity, why not? Not that I am advocating it mind you, but if it's not a femme thing, why hasn't she whisked you off to bed?"

"She's very self-contained, one of those rare breeds you meet that you feel never quite needs anyone permanently in her life. Self-controlled, selfcontained—all those things describe her."

"Lucky for us."

Jennifer looked at her. "Not lucky for us, because even if she's never a part of my life, I told you yesterday, I am not certain there is an *us*. Don't press too hard, Pam. I still don't know where I am in this."

They strolled the beach for hours, talking about Pam's efforts with the psychologist, their years together. Moments in those nearly 260 weeks they had been together that made both of them laugh. They took a long walk at Quoddy Head State Park and laughed some more about the fun of planting one's feet on the easternmost point of the continental United States.

Later, as Jennifer stood in the shower going back over the day, she realized that even with the fun, she had felt uncomfortable, and she couldn't figure out why. There had been discussions of reconciliation and regrets. Pam was leaving the next morning, Sunday, because there was a major meeting of her law partners Sunday night in Portland.

Although she had resisted the image, she had felt the physical tension between them growing, the physical draw that had been so much a part of their past life. She turned off the shower and wrapped a large pink towel around her. She looked at her reflection in the mirror and noted the dark circles under her eyes. It was decision time. They were going to have dinner at the Shoreside Inn and then talk some more. Pam had been contrite and acquiesced to Jennifer's fear that if there was too much pressure, she would explode.

As she opened the bathroom door she saw Pam coming up the stairs. Pam stopped and stared at Jennifer with a raw, naked want in her eyes.

Without word or sound Pam was against her, her lips and tongue drawing a pattern on her neck. Pam lifted her head and their gazes locked in an embrace of remembered lovemaking, then she lowered her mouth to Jennifer's. Her tongue was familiar as it explored the insides of Jennifer's mouth. Jennifer's tongue moved forward as Pam began to caress Jennifer's back.

"I've missed you, wanted you so badly." Pam's words were punctuated by the breathiness of her excitement. They were in Pam's room, the towel balled up next to Pam's running suit. Pam lay across her.

Jennifer remembered the physical thrill she had felt each time Pam's flesh was against her and wondered at that excitement. Pam was a skillful and attentive lover. She caressed Jennifer's breasts, and her hands roamed over her body while her mouth teased nipples that begged to be sucked.

Jennifer closed her eyes and thought of Kristan. She wondered what her lips would feel like. The touch of her skin. She tried to push the thought away, not wanting to betray this moment or to betray Kristan.

Pam's mouth was back on hers, their tongues doing the dance of familiarity. Jennifer raked her nails down Pam's back and felt her shiver with excitement. Then Pam was between her legs. Jennifer gasped as she felt the warm tongue, the heated breath. Her body raced closer to the first orgasm, then another.

Pam trailed more kisses up Jennifer's abdomen. "I've dreamed about this," she whispered as her mouth reached Jennifer's.

Jennifer's hands skillfully played along Pam's back as she rolled on top of her. Her fingers seemed to remember each spot on her body that made her moan. Jennifer buried her face against Pam's neck, determined to give herself over to making love to the woman whose body she had learned so well.

Afterwards they lay side by side. "Can I stay? I can skip the meeting tomorrow night." Pam rolled toward Jennifer and touched her cheek.

"No." Jennifer saw the hurt in Pam's eyes. "I still need time."

"We're so in sync, you saw how our bodies still speak to each other." Pam kissed Jennifer's nose.

Jennifer rolled onto her back. "Pam, I really do need time."

"I'm not asking you to come back. I can move here. I can start a practice. I expect the rubes here could use a good civil lawyer."

Jennifer sat up and reached for the towel that only hours before had been carelessly discarded. "I can't face those kinds of decisions right now."

"Is it because of the other woman?" Jennifer felt Pam's anger.

"No," said Jennifer, and knew that one word was the truth. She still felt a void, the void that in the past could be filled by their lovemaking. She sat on the edge of the bed.

Pam's fingers trailed up her back. Jennifer shivered. "We are so good together." Pam rolled over and kissed Jennifer's back. Jennifer felt herself collapsing back onto the bed.

❧

On Sunday morning, Jennifer eased herself away from Pam and into her own room. She slipped on a running suit and padded barefoot to the kitchen. She didn't grind any coffee, fearful it would wake Pam. She needed this time alone.

The lovemaking had gone on most of the night, and although it was warm and familiar, she still felt detached. Her body had responded to all the familiar touches, but her mind kept floating away, disconnected from what her body was feeling.

She had read that some women fantasized about someone else while making love with a familiar partner, but that had never happened to her before. No matter how much she had wanted to avoid thinking about Kristan, her face, her hands, the shape of her body crept into Jennifer's mind. She had definitely crossed some sort of Rubicon but was uncertain what it was or what it meant.

She heard Pam's feet on the stairs. She moved to the coffeepot.

"I missed you," Pam said as she hugged Jennifer from behind. "I want us to get back together. Whatever or however long it takes, that's what I want, and I think you want it too, but I know we have to take it one step at a time."

Jennifer kept her hands on the counter. She had no words to describe what she was feeling.

"I promised you space." Pam stepped back as if that move would emphasize her resolve. "I'm leaving this morning, though it's not what I want." Pam tried to add a lightness to her tone.

Jennifer hurried with breakfast, looking forward to the silence she would have after Pam left. A while later, Pam stared at her half-finished breakfast and then at Jennifer.

Jennifer could practically read her thoughts.

"I will fight for you."

"Wait a second, Pam. Don't go making those kinds of plans. The weekend has been great, but I need time to think this through. There won't be any fight for me. This will either happen or not."

"I know, but know this, Jennifer. I don't need time. I know what I want, and I am willing to change to have it."

Jennifer looked around, uncomfortable with the direction their conversation was going. "Let's take our time with this. I want this decision to be right."

"I will agree but with great reluctance." Pam stood up. Her packed bag was next to the back door. She turned and kissed Jennifer deeply. Her tongue was familiar, her hands warm. "I love you." She touched a finger to Jennifer's lips. "Focus on that," she said softly.

Jennifer watched as Pam's BMW left the driveway. What was she feeling? The ring of her phone interrupted her.

"I am just a few hundred feet from your driveway, and I already miss you."

Jennifer laughed. "Call me when you get to Portland. I want to know that you're safe."

"Ooh, now, I like that. Already worrying about me." The teasing helped relieve the tension. "I am going to call you every night."

Jennifer laughed. "I think that's a bit much, don't you?"

"Uh-uh. I think it's only the beginning. I'll call you tonight," Pam said. "And thank you."

Jennifer cradled the telephone. *The future. What is the future?*

Chapter 9

Kristan hunched down on one of the oak benches that looked like pews and waited for the court session to begin. She blinked at the clock: eight a.m., Monday. Too early. She hated early-morning court calls. She had left Jackie's at midnight. She had told Jackie about the encounter between Jennifer and the unidentified woman in the courthouse parking lot. Jackie said she had exaggerated the encounter, but every time Kristan focused on how Jennifer might be spending her weekend, she felt a pout coming on.

She watched the courtroom fill with all the Class D and C cases, drunk drivers, domestic assault charges. The flotsam and jetsam of the tides of justice. She was there for an arraignment of a twenty-one-year-old Bayport man.

She was happy when Toby finally plopped down next to her. He was in his uniform of the day—jeans, T-shirt and denim jacket. It was funny how his quiet style over the years had set the standard for the other reporters in town. Kristan practically looked like his clone. This morning she was wearing her favorite T-shirt. On the front were red and orange flames and one word: *Sinner.*

"Hey, darlin'." Kristan scooted across the pew.

"Look, we've got to have lunch. You've got to take some time from your schedule. We never get to visit anymore," he grumbled. He was red-headed with a matching red moustache. His charm came through in an affable relaxed manner and he had okay looks. Kristan often thought about that huge cross-section of Americans who had okay looks—her, Toby, Jackie. But not Jennifer. Shit, she thought, she was thinking about her again.

"Let's have lunch today. I've got time," she told Toby. "Are you here for the hate-crime case?"

"Yup, the jerk who kicked Indian ass in Bayport?"

Kristan cringed. "Toby, he kicked ass." Puzzlement at his use of the word *Indian* must have been written on her face. He knew that the tribe hated that word.

"I know. I know. I shouldn't have said 'Indian.' I didn't mean—"

Kristan read the embarrassment in his eyes.

"I know." She shifted in her seat. No lectures this morning. Toby had some of that subtle, undefined Jefferson County racism. It oozed from the soil, crawled up the roadways and spilled into homes. She changed the subject. "I hate early-morning hours."

"You should, you look terrible," Toby offered agreeably.

"Thank you," she enunciated slowly.

"No, I don't mean—" Toby blushed. "Yikes, I am having a bad morning." He shifted uncomfortably. "You look terrible in that—you don't look—ah, forget it. You know what I mean."

Kristan grinned. "Yeah." She paused and watched as more unsavory characters entered the courtroom. "What's the story on this guy?"

"Usual. You know the case. He pounded on a tribal member, state is calling it assault and a hate crime."

"Got that. I figured he wasn't from Bayport's finest." Kristan shifted her attention to Jennifer as she walked into the room carrying a square plastic box that looked like an old milk bottle crate. It was filled with case files. She looked tired. Kristan clenched her jaws. She was wavering between jealousy and disinterest. Jealousy was winning.

Jennifer did not look around. She set the files on the desk and bent over to speak with her secretary.

Toby's body stiffened. "She's really gorgeous."

"Uhm."

"She's not married? Lives alone," he said helpfully.

"So, you've been busy. Have you asked her out yet?" Kristan couldn't decide why she was irritated.

"Not yet, but soon." He grinned. "Have you checked her out?"

"No." Kristan could feel the heat rising in her neck. "I don't have a clue as to her pedigree or her living conditions," she snapped. She wondered if she should warn him, but was uncertain what to say. Jackie had argued that the woman in the parking lot was probably just a good friend, and she urged Kristan to wait for the real story instead of jumping to conclusions.

The door next to the judge's chamber opened and the court clerk entered. Elaine took her seat to the left of the judge's bench and tested the recording equipment. Tape recorders were cheaper than live court reporters, and Maine used that system in all the district courts. Elaine winked at Kristan as she arranged the papers on her desk. Kristan had learned that to be successful in the reporting business, you had to befriend all court clerks and secretaries. An occasional Dunkin' Donuts bribe also helped.

Kristan looked over at Jennifer. The new A.D.A. nervously tapped her pen against one of the files.

"All rise," the bailiff said. "Judge Barry McCarthy presiding."

"Be seated," the judge said.

"Nice butt," Toby whispered.

"What?"

"Nice butt," he whispered again and nodded toward the A.D.A.

"Toby, put your hormones on idle, will ya," Kristan whispered back. She knew he was pushing to get a rise out of her.

Kristan tuned out the first ten cases. There were the usual OUIs and operating after suspensions. Sprinkled in were a few domestic assaults and a couple of dog complaints. She watched Jennifer as she addressed the judge on each case. Her remarks were brief.

Kristan pushed her thoughts aside when the judge began her case. Chuck Gates stood along with his attorney, Jeffrey Bean. He was twenty-one years old and built like a football lineman. She had read the police report. It happened on Salem Street in Bayport, at a popular gathering place for young people. Around nine-thirty the night before, Eddie Soltree had been at the park when Gates yelled, "Hey, Redskin." Soltree ignored him. When Soltree left the park and headed downtown in the direction of Perry's Food Store, Gates had followed, confronted him and begun to hit him. Gates knocked Soltree to the ground and struck him in the face and head. Gates also kicked him while he was on the ground. The attack continued until someone pulled them apart. Gates was arrested, and Soltree was treated at Bailey's Cove Hospital for serious injuries to his ribs and kidneys.

Kristan tuned back in to the proceedings. Jennifer had finished her summary of the evidence the state had in the case.

"How do you plead?" the judge asked.

"Not guilty," Gates replied.

"Your recommendation?" McCarthy asked Jennifer.

"Well, Your Honor, I'd like bail set fairly high, at least five thousand dollars. The victim fears retaliation."

Gates's attorney whispered to his client, then told the judge he had no objections. Short and simple. Gates was handcuffed by a deputy and escorted from the courtroom. He would remain in jail until he or a family member could come up with his bail.

"Let's go ask her questions," Toby whispered, nodding toward Jennifer.

"It seems pretty straightforward. What would we ask her?" Kristan frowned.

"If she likes sex?" He grinned.

Kristan punched him. "Come on, he-man," she said, leading him out of the courtroom.

They caught up with Jennifer in the hallway leading to her office.

"Excuse me, any chance we can ask some questions about"— Kristan paused and looked mischievously at Toby—"the hate-crime case?" Kristan heard Toby's sigh.

"You can ask." Jennifer smiled. "What kinds of questions?"

"Questions like what kind of case do you have against him? If convicted how many years could he serve? The usual," Kristan said.

"And you?" Jennifer frowned at Toby.

"Ditto, what she said."

"Meet me in my office after the break. I should have some answers."

Lunch with Toby and the stop at the A.D.A.'s office had taken time, and Kristan had to type furiously to make her deadline. She had less than an hour to write, edit and file the story with Bangor.

"I wish I hadn't quit smoking," she told her computer. The phone rang. She watched the number appear on her caller ID. "Yes, Toby," she said to the black mouthpiece.

"Are you interested in her?"

"I don't know." This was the first time she and Toby had been interested in the same woman. She had never dealt with a male rival before, and she felt her aggressiveness ticking toward warp speed. She felt guilty she hadn't told him about the upcoming beachcombing day with Jennifer next weekend. But, she argued to herself, why should she—she might still call it off.

"Good, then why don't you put a good word in for me. Tell her what a heck of a nice guy I am."

"Not my job. You are on your own."

"Ah, come on, you're my pal."

"You're on your own. She's someone I'm going to have to work with, so you'll have to use your own little old charms to win her attention."

"I figured you'd tell her I was a sweetheart and not to resist my charms."

"Not a chance."

"Want to have dinner tonight?"

"Wow, you are bored. Nope, got to go to the store and head for home. I was out last night and I'm pooped."

"How about a drink Friday night, after my oldies show?"

"You're on. Look, babe, I'm on deadline, got to go."

"Oh," Toby interjected. "Don't forget we have a city council meeting tomorrow night."

"How could I forget?" Kristan hated council meetings.

Chapter 10

Kristan and Toby assumed their usual positions in the front row. It was the second Thursday of the month and time for the city council meeting.

Marcy Graham rushed in, her dangling purse slapping against her slim thighs. She had only moments before the meeting was to begin. The window was open, and Kristan could feel the slight breeze; it was a gentle May night. She was looking forward to Memorial Day and a long three-day weekend off.

"I thought I'd never get here, I had baby-sitter problems," the part-time neophyte reporter for the local weekly said.

"Why didn't you bring the babes along?" Kristan asked.

"Bite your tongue. This is the only quiet I get."

"Probably would liven up the meetings."

Toby leaned around Kristan and asked Marcy, "You coming tonight?"

"Only for about an hour. Do I ever need a drink." Marcy stuck her car keys in her purse and pulled out a tape recorder and her notepad. She placed her camera on the floor next to her chair.

The city manager was the first official to enter the council chambers. She stopped at Kristan's chair. "You have a moment to see me after the meeting?"

"Sure."

"Why don't you join all of us for a drink tonight?" Marcy invited.

"I'd like to, but . . ." Sally paused. "It's not that I wouldn't like a drink, but it wouldn't be good for me to be seen with you guys." She grinned. "Could ruin my reputation."

Three of the councilors walked into the room, stopping to chat with various people as they made their way to the council table. Sally greeted them.

"Disreputable bunch that we are," Kristan interjected as she waved to the councilors.

"Right." Sally stopped talking when she saw Mayor Jasper Green in the doorway.

"Good evening, mayor," she said as she moved toward the small desk to the right of the council seats.

The mayor nodded to the city manager and looked at the clock on the wall. It was just seconds before seven. He leaned over to confer with the city clerk, then picked up his gavel and called the meeting to order.

Kristan looked at the agenda. She noted that Francis Gardner was scheduled to address the council about the courthouse parking lot. Usually the district attorney did not attend city council meetings, but it was his job to notify the councilors if there were city-county problems. People on city business were parking their vehicles in the county courthouse lot. There was barely enough room for people there on courthouse business, and trial days were nuts with potential jurors having to park blocks away. So the state was going to post the parking lot, and the city police would enforce removal of errant vehicles.

Kristan looked around to see if Francis had arrived and wondered if Jennifer would accompany him. She was disappointed that neither he nor Jennifer was there. She pulled out her monthly calendar and studied her schedule for the rest of May.

The councilors droned on about solid-waste issues and bid openings. The public works department needed a new dump truck. Kristan noted that a request for a new police cruiser was absent. She shook her head. The police chief was going to be unhappy.

She heard Toby sigh and knew even before she looked toward the door that Jennifer had entered the council room. She noted the forest green suit and the pale green blouse. Jennifer smiled at Kristan, or maybe at Toby, she wasn't sure.

"Yikes, I have got to ask her out," Toby whispered to Kristan.

"Is that . . ." Marcy nodded toward Jennifer, who had moved to the back of the room.

"Yeah, and what a knockout." Toby rolled his eyes.

"Down, boy." Kristan jabbed him in the side with her elbow.

"Be still, my beating heart." Toby fanned himself with his reporter's notebook.

Kristan shook her head. "Such dramatics," she whispered.

"I ain't acting." Toby grinned.

Marcy leaned forward. "She's cute."

Kristan frowned at Marcy.

"*Cute* is not the word, she is a knockout, and what a great personality," Toby whispered.

"How do you know?"

"Since that memorable breakfast morning at Tippys, I've stopped over at Francis's office several times during the past few weeks. You know, checking on cases, seeing if there was anything newsworthy." Toby drew out "newsworthy."

Smack! The gavel hit the table.

Kristan, Toby and Marcy jumped. "We would like the attention of the fourth estate." Jasper looked at Kristan over his half-moon glasses.

"Sorry, mayor." Kristan frowned at Toby and Marcy. She shifted in her seat and glanced behind her, and her gaze ran smack into Jennifer's smirk.

After the meeting, Kristan said to Toby and Marcy, "I need to stop at my office. I'll meet you at Three Sisters in about ten minutes." She let herself in to her dark office and ignored the blinking message light on her answering machine.

She took off her fanny pack and set her carrying case with her recorder, camera and notebooks on the chair in front of her desk. She took her wallet out of her pouch and stuffed a $20 bill in the pocket of her Levi's.

The front door slammed. She frowned and waited as someone walked down the short hallway to the inside door. She was surprised that it was Jennifer.

"Hi. I saw your light."

Kristan leaned against her desk. "Hi." She no doubt looked more relaxed than she felt. "Well, how did you enjoy your first meeting of Bailey's Cove City Council?"

"Not quite on a par with anything I've ever seen before. Usually we don't have to attend, but Francis asked me to join him, so I did. Are they usually that boring?"

"Naw, every now and than there's an issue that stirs their passion, and the next thing you know they're fighting and screaming."

Jennifer walked around Kristan's small office. She stopped at the bulletin board that most reporters seemed to have fixed to their walls. On it were rejected photographs and nametags from longforgotten meetings, odds and ends, souvenirs. Kristan silently watched her.

"I'm looking forward to our beachcombing trip on Saturday." Jennifer turned and smiled. "I was wondering, what time?"

Kristan made a rapid review of when the tide would be out. "Nine?" Yikes, she thought, now she's going to think I use only monosyllabic sentences.

"Good."

"I'll put together a picnic breakfast."

"What can I bring?"

"Nothing. I've got it covered."

Jennifer reached over and straightened one of the pictures on the bulletin board. "Great." She turned back toward Kristan. "Well, I don't want to keep you from your night out with the other reporters. So I'll see you then."

"How'd you know about my night out with the reporters?"

Jennifer's smile was self-confident. "You're not the only one in the city who has sources."

"Ah."

Jennifer stepped toward Kristan, reached out and adjusted the collar on her shirt. Kristan felt her knees sag. "It was slightly askew. You want to look nice at the bar," she said, her hand still on the collar. "See you Saturday," she said softly.

Kristan braced her palms against her desk. "Right."

Jennifer left as quietly as she had arrived.

Avoiding, Kristan thought. She knew she was attracted to Jennifer but was running scared. She thought about all those years with Patti, her only long-term relationship. Somewhere toward the end boredom set in and she recalled those trips to Bangor and the weekends she fooled around. Patti found out and said bye-bye. Now her ex was living in Boston and in a very happy relationship with another woman. Kristan stared at her reflection in the window. She had not found anyone else who had piqued her interest until now. "Ignore it," she said aloud. She wanted the sound of her voice to convince her, but she wasn't certain she could hold her attraction for Jennifer in check. She was uneasy about the direction their conversations were going. The innocent but flirting eyes. There were women who flirted with everyone. And what about the other woman?

She turned off the lights, locked her office and walked the half block to Three Sisters. She liked the atmosphere there. It was owned by three women, not related, who had grown up in the city.

The bar was dark, illuminated only by signs that advertised things like Red Baron and Miller. A single fluorescent bulb highlighted the dark green felt of the pool table. On Thursday nights after the council meetings, the press and a few city workers had the bar to themselves. Toby was going on about the meeting and the mayor.

"Yeah, but who do we get to replace him?" Kristan frowned at her seltzer and lime. "He is a known commodity. You can feel comfortable with him. No surprises, nothing out of the ordinary."

"The guy is a drone. It is his way or the doorway. Come on, Kristan." Toby emphasized his words with his bottle of beer. "We desperately need some new blood in city government. The guy is an albatross, a leech, sucking the city's blood into his body."

"Yuk." Marcy took a swig of her beer. "Could we be a little less graphic?"

"But he has the city's interest at heart." Kristan defended the mayor.

"Speaking of heart." Toby put his hand over his chest. "Did you see my heart enter warp speed when that warm, wonderful, welcome body entered."

"The new A.D.A." Marcy grinned. "I thought I heard your hormones slip into overdrive. Have you talked with her much?" she asked Kristan.

"Yes, but I haven't been hanging around the D.A.'s office looking for news like some people have." She punched Toby in the arm just as he raised the bottle of beer to his lips. Beer dripped down his chin and onto his shirt.

He mopped his shirt with the tiny bar napkin. "She warms my heart."

Kristan did not smile. "Anything in a skirt warms your heart."

"Foul, Kristan, foul."

"Come on you guys, quit squabbling. Is Francis going out the door?"

"Not so you'd notice. When I was over there," Toby said, the beer bottle inches from his mouth as he watched for any more abrupt movements by Kristan, "he was in the thick of it. Talking with cops, victims, you name it. It seems as though they have a bigger caseload since Jennifer signed on."

"Bigger caseload?" Kristan said. "Or fewer pleas."

"Good point." Toby stroked his stubbly chin. "Maybe both."

"Well, it's possible. I know Francis has been swamped and has accepted a lot of plea bargains. It's rare for him to take anything to court anymore. His favorite sentence seems to be ten days, all suspended," Marcy said cynically.

Kristan felt more comfortable now that the conversation had shifted away from Jennifer. She looked up as the door opened, and Billy and David Robinson walked in. She frowned. She noticed that Tina wasn't with them. Billy saw Kristan and hesitated in the doorway. He said something to David, who looked over at Kristan and waved. She did not wave back.

Billy greeted others as he walked across the bar to her table. "Hi." He included the group in his greeting.

"Hey, man, join us," Toby said. He hadn't noticed Kristan's silence.

"Thanks, but I'm with Davey. But catch you later." Billy turned back toward the bar. Kristan noticed the shot and beer in front of Davey, with another sitting on the bar apparently waiting for Billy. Kristan sensed Billy's discomfort at seeing her, and she was enjoying it.

"How's Tina?" she called after him.

Billy turned back around. "Great. She said something about having lunch with you. You should call her."

"I will." She stared at him.

He shifted on his feet, and then Davey's laugh drew his attention to the bar. "Gotta go." Davey had a fistful of money in his hand and was buying drinks for everyone.

Toby and Marcy watched Billy walk away. Kristan looked down at her drink.

"What's going on?" Marcy asked Kristan.

"What do you mean?"

"I can read frigid. I thought you guys were friends."

"Well." Kristan scratched her eyebrow. "Just let's say—right now I think Billy should be home with his wife and kids. But t'aint none of my business. Right?"

"It really isn't," Marcy agreed. "I'd heard he's been out and about. Nothing with women, just hanging out."

"I can understand it," Toby interjected. "Men sometimes get restless."

"That's pretty sexist." Marcy frowned at her friend.

"I just mean—"

"I know what you mean," Kristan said quietly. "But I would expand that. Some people get restless." She thought about those nights in Bangor. "So I guess he isn't doing anything anyone hasn't done, but when it's your best friend's husband you tend to hang objectivity on a lamp post."

Chapter 11

It had been a busy Friday, and now Jennifer looked forward to this day and her picnic with Kristan. She was pleased to escape the mental burden she had fallen under thinking about Pam. She couldn't get a handle on what was going to happen between them, but she knew things were off sync. Pam had told her, during one of the many telephone conversations they'd had since she left, that she had felt absolutely exulted during their time together.

Jennifer had felt absolute bone-crunching boredom. It had taken her days to articulate how she felt, and on the nights when she and Pam talked on the telephone, she was eager to get off.

She frowned at the mirror in her bathroom. Pam had called the night before, ostensibly to ask about a case she was handling, but she was pushing for them to get together again and wanted Jennifer to come to Portland. Jennifer had refused, again using work as an excuse. Unfortunately, Pam rarely took no for an answer. Decision time would come soon.

She studied herself in the mirror. Even though she had slept well for the first time in weeks, the dark circles under her eyes still looked like black ashes. Worry lines creased her forehead. Thirty-two years old, and she felt eighty. Exercise and a newfound interest? Maybe that was the answer.

She was attracted to Kristan but uncertain where Kristan's head was. Never once had there been a word or suggestion of something other than a comfortable camaraderie. She had been careful in the questions she had asked about her. Even the gossipers seemed to preface everything with, "She's honest and she's ethical."

During one such conversation, Jennifer's secretary had hinted that Kristan used to live with a woman, but Brenda offered few details. Jennifer thought about the Down East reaction to anyone who lived an alternative lifestyle. If people here liked you, a protective force field would surround you. You might be a queer, but you were their queer.

She heard a soft knock on the door and felt her spirits lighten as she opened it.

"Good morning, counselor." Kristan handed her a box of Dunkin' Donuts and a cup of coffee.

"Please not 'counselor.' If I hear that word one more time I'll scream," Jennifer said with a laugh.

Kristan grinned. "I expect you skipped eating. I was going to take you to breakfast, but I thought it would be nice to go sit on a rock and eat breakfast. The only bother will be the seagulls, but they are honest in their interest, they just want us for the food."

"Good idea. I'll get my jacket."

"It's cool but comfortable out. In a few more hours the sun will be just right, and we can take off our clothes."

Jennifer turned to look at Kristan, who immediately blushed.

"Our jackets," she stammered. "And sweatshirts," she added lamely.

Jennifer laughed. "Come in. I'll be right down."

❧

They drove in comfortable silence back through the city and down a side road. Kristan pulled into a long driveway that wound through hundreds of green balsam pines.

It was cool, but Jennifer opened her window anyway and inhaled. "God, I love that smell. It always reminds me of Christmas."

"That's what I love most about this area. People work all year and spend thousands of dollars to vacation in Maine, and we lucky few have it yearround. It's a gift, a real gift," Kristan said.

"Do people tip here?" Jennifer asked, referring to the balsam boughs that wreath makers gather during the fall.

"For a few years there were problems, but that was resolved. Now I allow a few careful people to come in and tip and leave a reserve for the next year. They pretty well keep the tree rapists at bay."

"You live here?" Jennifer said as a large white Cape loomed into her view. She could see the dark blue of the ocean in the deep distance. "This is breathtaking."

Kristan stopped the car and leaned slightly toward her to look out the passenger window. Jennifer could feel Kristan's sleeve against her arm and she shivered.

"It's beautiful, isn't it," Kristan said solemnly. "I remember the first time I saw it, I was just a kid, and I knew that someday I would own it." She drew back, shifted and pulled the car the rest of the way up the driveway.

Although Jennifer felt her own ocean view was beautiful and unique, she hadn't been prepared for this. "Give me a minute to take it all in," she said as they parked near the house.

Kristan retrieved the coffee and doughnuts from the back seat, and waited quietly as Jennifer scanned the view.

"Let's take the path," Kristan offered.

Jennifer followed Kristan for what seemed like a mile. The path rose and fell, twisted and turned. She heard the song of the chickadees; there must have been hundreds of them. The wind ruffled the needles of the thick stand of pine trees.

She heard the breakers before she saw them smashing against the shale cliffs. As they rounded a bend in the trail, Kristan stopped and Jennifer stood just inches behind her. She could feel Kristan's warmth and again wondered at her attraction to this woman.

She eyed the outcropping of rocks and inlets that butted up against the shore. The sun cast black and tan shadows across craggy cliffs inviting exploration. Jennifer wanted to touch the warm rocks, finger the sharp edges and run her palms over the smooth angles that fell away to the shore.

On the right there was a small sandy beach with a sprinkling of red and yellow rocks as well as a smattering of white quartz. The only evidence of human activity was a rough wooden bench partially hidden by large white birch trees. "Your bench?" she asked.

"It was here when I bought it. At first I was going to remove it—it somehow disturbed the balance—but then I sat and—" Kristan paused, almost embarrassed. "I felt this ascendancy of my spirit. It's the most perfect spot to watch everything—the waves, the beach, the cliffs, the seals, the whales. It was right. I expect that's why somebody put it there."

"Can we sit there?"

"Of course." Kristan laughed. "But first let's sit on the rocks and have breakfast. I don't want you to collapse." She scrambled across the rocks, never once losing her footing. She balanced the coffee and doughnuts perfectly across the uneven rocks.

Jennifer was a little less sure. Her hiking boots were clumsy on the sharp shale as she stepped between crevices and stumbled over uneven terrain. "You have such confidence," she said to Kristan.

"Confidence? Oh." Kristan gestured toward the terrain. "No, a friend suggested I was part mountain goat."

"That sounds accurate."

"I thought you'd agree." She opened a large coffee and handed it to Jennifer. "Coffee, two creams, no sugar."

"Very good," Jennifer said appreciatively. "And for you?"

"Hot chocolate." Kristan touched her paper cup to Jennifer's. "To a quiet day."

"I will happily drink to that."

Kristan handed her the bag of doughnuts. "Here, there's something for everyone, including the seagulls."

Jennifer pulled out a chocolate-covered Kahlua cream and licked the stickiness from her fingers as she felt Kristan watching her. A soft shudder moved up her spine.

"Do you come down here often?" She handed the bag back to Kristan. Calm down, she told herself.

"As often as my job allows. When I retire, I'll be here every day." Kristan turned to look at her house that sat like a small dot against the blue skies. "I have a great view, but there's nothing like the walk through the woods. You can hear the ocean before you see it, and then you come around that bend and wow! There it is. I've lived here for ten years, but each time it's a brand new experience. Something like the first time you fall in love with someone. It's that first time over and over again, pure perfection."

"I like that. I think everyone can relate to those first moments when you fall in love."

"Yeah. But unlike the drudgery of a relationship, this—" Kristan's tone was cynical as she gestured toward the expanse. "Stays new."

Jennifer frowned. "Drudgery?"

"Don't you think day-to-day living bogs down into drudgery?"

"Probably, if the day-to-day living is with the wrong person, but with the right person, it's warm, comforting, safe," Jennifer said, quietly remembering her first few years with Pam. She liked the nights around the fireplace, books resting in their laps.

Kristan stared at her. "And have you had warm, comforting, safe?"

"Yes." Jennifer felt the heat in her cheeks. "Yes, I have. For a while anyway."

"The woman at the courthouse?"

"You saw her? Of course you saw her. Let's not dance around the issue." Jennifer cocked her eyebrow. "Yes, for a time it was warm and comforting."

"What happened?"

Jennifer shifted on the rocks. She wasn't sure how much she wanted to reveal.

Kristan held up her hand. "Don't answer. I was out of bounds, even beyond the scope of a nosy reporter. I'm not going to pry."

"Just let's say that we were two people with very diverse goals and needs. And different attitudes about monogamy. Now it's my turn to ask you a question?"

"Shoot."

"Do you really see relationships as a drudgery?"

"For me. Not for everyone. I've made bad choices. My friend Jackie had the perfect relationship. I was jealous." Kristan paused. "Not that I resented her happiness, but I was jealous that she had fallen in love with the right person. They were perfectly matched. You felt like you were always glimpsing the ruling spirit of happiness every time you were with them." She stared at the ocean for a long time. "Then Marianne died. You know what's funny? If the right person came along, she'd fall in love again. That's the part I don't understand."

"I think I can understand it. It seems to me that if someone has found perfection in a relationship, they would believe they could recapture it."

"Maybe."

"You seem doubtful."

"Once you've tasted perfection, it seems to me that everything else would be second best."

"Very cynical, reporter."

"Not on purpose. I've had two relationships, and believe me, although I thought I'd found perfection, I hadn't." Kristan looked obliquely at Jennifer as if a stubborn cell in her brain was demanding an answer. "I know I said it would be out of bounds, but what happened to you and the woman in the parking lot?"

Jennifer crossed her legs at the ankles and leaned back on her hands. She thought about what to say, where to begin. Her coffee cup was warm, held solidly between her thighs. "I figured you saw us in the parking lot. I saw your car parked out there that night." Jennifer took a deep breath. "I met Pam in law school. We lived together for five years."

Kristan blushed. "Are you still involved with the law school woman?" she asked.

"I don't know." Frustrated, Jennifer rubbed a hand over her tired brow. "She wants to be. That's all we talked about while she was here, but I don't feel quite as committed to the idea of a relationship as she is. And you?" Jennifer leaned back on her elbows. "You've neglected to mention gender."

"Women." Kristan stared down at her hands.

Jennifer wanted to ask more questions, but Kristan drew a force field of silence around herself.

"Come on, I promised you some great beachcombing, and I always keep my promises." Kristan reached for Jennifer's hand and pulled her to a standing position. She stepped back from her just as quickly.

The bounty was plentiful. Their jacket pockets were stuffed with seashells and special rocks that could not be left behind.

Kristan led the way back to where they started. During the climb up and down the rocks and the exploration of the inlets, Jennifer guessed they had walked about five miles. She was tired but felt relaxed for the first time in months. "This was great, Kristan, thanks."

"Just what the doctor ordered."

"Was it your doctor friend who suggested we go beachcombing?"

"Yup."

"Would you have thought of it on your own?"

Kristan pushed her hand through her hair. "Probably not for ten or fifteen years. I'm pretty shy."

Jennifer stood looking at her, taking in the slim shoulders and hips, the strong hands that only hours before had pulled her to a standing position. She liked Kristan's height, at least a head taller than her. "Shy?" she repeated.

"I know, I know." Kristan laughed. "I could walk into a room and ask the President of the United States the most piercing and intimate questions possible, but in this personal relationship stuff, I'm pretty shy."

"Well, that's good to know."

Kristan looked at her quizzically, unsure how to respond. "Would you like to sit on the bench? I took the liberty of stocking some supplies."

"I'd like that."

They sat for several minutes staring at the beach. "This is eerily beautiful," Jennifer said quietly. She felt really at peace.

"You know, I sit here, and I can really concentrate on all those abstract concepts that seem to elude me in everyday life. Like who we are and where we are going." Kristan paused. "And what I want to be when I grow up."

Jennifer paused. "And what do you want to be when you grow up?"

"Don't know. Not a reporter." Kristan's eyes sparkled. She leaned back, her hands grasping the edge of the rough board they sat on.

Jennifer felt the moment suddenly break between them. She looked down and was surprised to see her hands clasped together. Her palms were sweaty.

"Too much heavy stuff on a day when I promised you nothing but sun and relaxation." Kristan reached behind her and pulled out a worn knapsack. She dug around inside and pulled out two carefully wrapped objects. She handed them to Jennifer. "Open them."

"Crystal wineglasses." Jennifer held them up. The Waterford sparkled in the sunlight. They were beautiful. "Very nice."

Kristan turned and leaned into the trees. Jennifer looked at the lines of her back and the way they curved down across her butt. She sighed deeply.

"I have—" Kristan laughed as she righted herself. "I have my own private cooler. There's a stream back here with this tiny pool that keeps everything cold. This, madam"—Kristan held up the icy bottle of wine—"goes with the two glasses. And . . ." She again reached back into the trees. She pulled out plastic bags and cans dripping with icy water. "We have lobster rolls, made special this morning. Fresh smoked salmon and a blockbuster dessert—Ben and Jerry's, Cherry Garcia."

Jennifer laughed. She set the crystal glasses on the bench and touched Kristan's arm. "Thank you. This is really special."

"You're welcome." She paused then said, "Enough of this maudlin look at life. Let's eat." She skillfully popped the cork from the wine.

Jennifer lay against the rocks, the sun in her face. She had slept deeply but now could feel Kristan stirring near her. She opened her eyes and blinked at the sun. "I wonder what time it is."

"About four."

"You're kidding." She raised herself to her elbows. "How long have I been asleep?"

"We've been asleep, I'd say, at least two hours."

"I promised Francis I would stop by." She looked straight at the sun. "I really don't want this to end. I haven't felt this relaxed in months."

Kristan shifted on the rocks, resting her head in her hand. "We can do it again." She looked away. She seemed suddenly depressed. She stood up and brushed the white chalk of the rocks off her pants. She reached out to Jennifer and pulled her up.

Jennifer impulsively hugged her. "Thank you," she said, her breath against Kristan's neck.

Kristan held her at arm's length. "This really was my pleasure."

"Would you have dinner with me?"

"I'd like that. We have some really great restaurants."

"I was thinking more of cooking spaghetti. I hope you like Italian."

"Love it. When?"

"Wednesday night, six?"

"Thanks."

They were silent on their walk back to Kristan's car. Kristan put the knapsack on her deck before she returned to the car. Jennifer sat and waited for her, thinking about the day. She felt the attraction. Now, she wondered, what was she to do about Pam?

There was little conversation on the trip back to Jennifer's house. Kristan pulled into the driveway and turned to say good-bye. Jennifer leaned forward and quietly kissed her lips. "Thank you." Then she jumped out, waved and headed for her front door. "See you Wednesday night."

Chapter 12

Kristan was uncertain what the protocol was in a situation like this. Should she take flowers, wine? It had been a long time since she had had dinner with someone other than close friends and she didn't quite know how to act. She and Jennifer had talked often on the telephone. Their weekend walk was still a very present memory.

"Ah, Jacks." She shifted the receiver and rested it on her left shoulder. "When you go to dinner, do you take wine, flowers, or wine and flowers?"

"Well, it depends."

"On what?" Kristan demanded.

"On who you are having dinner with."

"Oh."

"So who are you having dinner with?"

"Uhm."

"The new A.D.A."

"Uhm."

"What is this, wordsmith? Are you retreating to nonverbal communication? You sound guttural."

"I've never sounded guttural in my life," Kristan huffed as she shifted the receiver to her other ear. "I just don't want you to tease me."

"Would I do that?"

"You bet. In a second. So answer the question. It wasn't that hard. Wine, flowers, wine and flowers?"

"I understand she's serving spaghetti, so a nice red wine."

"Wait a minute, how'd you know that?"

Jackie chuckled. "Oh, I've got my sources." That was the second time Kristan had heard those same words in the last few days.

"Jackson, I demand to know where you got your information."

"Nope."

"I mean it."

"Ah . . . I think flowers would be a little too much of a statement, just a nice red wine."

"Okay, but who told you?"

"You argue, you're going to be late. She said six p.m."

A strangled noise erupted from Kristan's throat. "Where'd you learn that?"

"Same source," Jackie answered matter-of-factly. Then Kristan heard the distinctive click. She also heard Jackie's great hefty throaty laugh just before she hung up.

Kristan slipped on her jacket. She reached for her keys and the door just as the telephone rang. She glared at the instrument. "No, I am not going to answer it. I am not going to answer it." She snatched up the receiver. "What," she barked crossly.

"Hi. Bad time?"

"Not for you, Tina. Sorry, I thought it was one of my assignment editors."

"Well, I had a free night. Billy has taken the kids in to enjoy a burger barf special, and I was wondering if you wanted to have dinner."

"I—"

Tina rushed on. "We haven't talked since you helped me get the job at the school, and I wanted to tell you about some of the things that have been happening to me."

"I'm already invited to dinner tonight, otherwise you know I'd jump at the chance. But how about tomorrow?"

"I doubt I could get Billy to take care of the kids two nights in a row." Tina paused.

"What's wrong, pal?" Kristan set her keys and jacket down and perched on the back of her sofa.

"Just things." Tina started to say something and then stopped. "Nothing of crisis proportion. So who are you having dinner with?"

Well, at least it wasn't all over the city, Kristan thought, even though Jackie seemed to know all about it. "The new assistant district attorney." Kristan waited for the response.

"I hear she's bright and good at what she does."

"Seems so."

"Well, I won't keep you."

"Look." Kristan didn't want to let her go even though she noted that the clock was creeping closer to six. "Let's have lunch tomorrow. I'll carve out a couple of hours."

"I'd like that. You really are a pal."

"Well, so are you."

After she hung up she frowned at the telephone. The usually bubbly Tina was not herself, and she felt guilty putting her off.

The trip to the liquor store took longer than expected. For someone who usually was happy with Beringers, the rows of more elegant wines were a puzzle. She liked Maine better before the California wine companies found it. In the old days, there was one shelf, neatly lined with a few reds and whites. Now there were shelves of wine and prices ranged from really cheap to $30 a bottle. She wanted a dry red, but not so dry that it made your jaws clench. She reached for a medium-priced red. Kristan felt the hand on her shoulder and turned quickly.

"Jacks."

"Kristan, I saw your car." Jackie's face was grave and preoccupied. "There's been a bad accident." As the city's medical examiner she was only called to an accident if there was a death.

"Where?" Kristan set the bottle back on the shelf and could feel adrenaline shifting into high gear.

"Out on Route One, just before the Bailey's Cove/Fordland town line," Jackie said over her shoulder as she headed back out through the open door.

Kristan yanked off her jacket. She could feel sweat gathering under her arms. "Sorry, Jake, no wine tonight," she said to the confused clerk as she ran to her car.

She saw Jackie's red Mustang kick up dust as it zigzagged out of the parking lot. Kristan jumped into her own vehicle, ignoring the seat belt. She threw it into reverse and screeched out of the parking lot. She stomped down on the accelerator. Her reporter's bag was in the backseat. She never left home without it.

Oh no, she thought, Jennifer would have to wait. She silently chewed herself out. For years now she had considered getting a cell phone but had resisted it because being in the car was her only time alone.

She would assess the situation, get a few pictures and then leave. She'd leave Jennifer's number with the cops so they could call her with the details. No, she couldn't do that. More people didn't have to know that she and Jennifer were having dinner together. It was just a few minutes after six p.m. She knew it would take the cops hours to clear the scene.

She decided she could get enough information at the scene to call in to her assignment editors. She'd only be a few minutes late to Jennifer's.

She felt better once she had resolved how she would handle all her obligations. She could follow up with a more detailed story the next day. It was May. No doubt the accident involved tourists, so the cops wouldn't be ready to release names until they had notified the next of kin.

Kristan approached the scene. Cars were pulled off on either side of the road. Gawkers were standing around a pile of metal that Kristan could not identify. No blue lights, so that meant she was ahead of the cops. No barricades or yellow tape delineating an accident scene. She parked behind the farthest car. She saw Jackie's red Mustang several feet ahead of her.

Kristan grabbed her camera and notebook and ran toward the scene. She saw the dog first, lying on its side, blood running from its mouth. She stopped and looked around for Jackie and saw her kneeling over someone who was lying next to what was once a car. It was a crumpled tangled mass of metal. Kristan stopped. Jackie looked up and shook her head. Kristan blinked.

It was Billy, his arms and legs at odd angles with his body.

"This is not a tourist, this is . . ." Kristan looked around. She heard the wrenching of metal as the passenger door was forced open.

"He needs some air," someone said.

Kristan almost stopped functioning. She heard a child cry, "I want my mommy." The cry was the mournful sound of pain. Ashley was whimpering.

A man was speaking in a calm voice trying to comfort him. It was Sean McLadden, a paramedic. "Doc, we need you over here," Sean called.

"Jackie, where is Kelsey?" Kristan was having difficulty processing the scene.

"Over there."

Kristan looked to where she had nodded, then back at Jackie. Jackie quietly shook her head. On the side of the road, a blanket covered a small mound. The seat she had been sitting in was on the ground next to her.

"Oh, no." Kristan fought back the tears.

Kristan looked back at the twisted metal. Jackie had moved over to Ashley. The roof on the driver's side had been peeled back like a layer of dead skin. Part of the roof just hung at the back of the car, occasionally moving as people tried to reach inside to help the boy.

The paramedic had stepped aside to make room for Jackie. He grabbed Kristan's arm, trying to put himself between Kristan and the back of the car. "Don't look."

But she had already seen Dusty in the backseat, and she walked over to the side of the road and vomited.

"Stay detached," Kristan told herself. "Stay detached."

She looked back and saw that Jackie had squeezed her large frame into the mass of metal. Her hands were red from the blood she wiped from Ashley's eyes and nose.

"Get my bag," she yelled. Roger Simpson, who worked at the local Wal-Mart and was a volunteer firefighter, handed it through the roof. "Somebody throw a blanket over that side." She nodded to where Dusty still sat.

Kristan walked to the front of the car. She stepped around a large object, the Nash's engine. What was it doing outside the car? Kristan's thoughts were a jumble. This was not the way it was supposed to be. She shouldn't know these people. She bit down on her bottom lip and fought back another gag. She pushed her way between the even bigger crowd. "How is he?"

Jackie shrugged. Shook her head.

"Has anyone called Tina?" Kristan's voice sounded as though it was in another room, distant even to her own ears. She looked at faces in the crowd.

"Yeah."

Kristan wasn't sure who had answered.

"I want my mommy." It was Ashley's voice between tiny little hurt sobs. She could hear Jackie's quiet voice. A disembodied calm floated over the scene.

Kristan heard the sirens before she saw the blue lights. Ambulances followed the cop cars.

The chief pushed through the crowd. He assessed the scene and yelled at Sean and Roger to assist him with crowd control.

"All right, people, you have to move back." His arms outstretched, he pushed into the center of the crowd. People melted into the background. More cops arrived.

Kristan stepped away from the Nash. It wasn't until she had turned to her right that she saw the large black Chevrolet convertible, its once sleek nose a tangle. Fire had gutted the interior. The steel spines that had supported the closed convertible top looked like separated ribs. There was nothing left of the white canvas.

No one was in the vehicle. She walked toward the car. David Robinson was walking around in front of the car mumbling, dabbing at his bloody face with what looked like a dirty car blanket. There was another blanket over a body in front of the car.

The air was filled with sirens and people shouting for gurneys. Most of the crowd had been pushed farther back from the scene. Kristan wondered how much evidence had been trampled during the first few moments after the accident when so many had rushed to help. She knew she had trampled on evidence and had probably even thrown up on some.

As she walked around the periphery of the scene, she gulped cool night air into her lungs.

Kristan saw Jackie walking next to the gurney carrying Ashley. The doctor followed him into the back of the ambulance. The doors slammed shut and the siren signaled its rush to the hospital.

Then she saw a blue car pull up and Tina was sitting in the passenger seat. Kristan rushed to her.

"My babies, my babies." Tina had the door open before the car had come to a stop. Her brother, Tommy Stickney, was trying to steer clear of the crowd and grab for Tina's shirt at the same time. Tina stumbled as she jumped out of the moving car. Her knees went down on the road; her chin hit the door panel. Her palms skidded along the pavement. There was no cry of pain; she was clearly beyond feeling.

The chief saw the vehicle and was the first to grab Tina, pulling her to her feet. She tried to break and run toward the Nash, but he pulled her hard against his chest.

Tina's fists pummeled Joey, smashing at his face. She was all over him, her arms, fists, feet. She pulled at his hands trying to break his grip. He held her away to avoid her blows but did not let go of her. She looked like a recalcitrant child trying to escape the firm hold of a stern parent.

"Please let me go." Her voice pleaded; her eyes begged.

Cops ran to help the chief. "It's okay." He backed them off with a look.

Joey looked over at Kristan.

"Tina," Kristan said softly. Her voice still sounded as though it belonged to someone else. Her ears heard, but her mind was unfocused. "Tina, come with me." Kristan searched for words. She seemed to be out of her body; it was someone else talking to Tina. "Tina, we have to go see Ashley."

"Ashley?" Tina turned to Kristan. "Where's my baby?"

"Tina, let me take you to the hospital. Ashley's at the hospital," Kristan said as she tried to ease her toward her brother's car.

"My babies? They're at the hospital." Tina looked puzzled. Her face was a study in steadfast grief.

Jennifer looked at the clock. Five minutes had passed since the last time she looked. Seven p.m. At six-thirty she had turned off the heat under the spaghetti sauce. Her jaw was clenched. Well, this was a first, she thought: she stood me up. She bit on her thumbnail, her irritation growing with each bite. The telephone interrupted her gnawing. She was uncertain how she would handle Kristan's unexcused lateness.

"Yes?"

"Jennifer? Francis." She heard the hesitancy, the unexpected slowness of speech.

"Is something wrong?"

"Jennifer, there's been a bad accident. We have a lot of people dead. You need to go over and look at the scene, get a feel for it. You're going to handle this one."

"Where?"

"On Route One, going toward Fordland."

"Francis, are you all right?"

"No—yes."

"You know them?" The question need not have been asked. Jennifer barely heard the quiet yes before the line went dead.

Chapter 13

Kristan sat next to Tina in the car and put her arm around her shoulders. Tina wiped the blood on her hands off on her jeans, and Kristan struggled for the right words to say but realized there were none.

Tina grabbed at the door handle before the car stopped outside the emergency entrance. Kristan held onto her shoulder and tried to stop her. "Tina," she murmured.

Tommy looked over. "Tina, they might not let you see Ashley right away."

Tina climbed over Kristan and half ran, half stumbled to the door. "I have to see him."

Sandra McKinney was standing at the nurses' station and when she saw the commotion, she used her substantial body to block the entrance to the treatment cubicles. "Tina, the doctor is with him right now," she said gently. "You need to sit down," she said when she saw Tina's bloody palms. "Come in here." She nodded to a small room with a curtain pulled around it. "We've got to clean those hands. Why don't you two wait out here and I'll take care of her," Sandra said to Tommy and Kristan.

"Will you take me to him?" Tina asked as she followed Sandra like an obedient puppy.

"Tell me." Tommy's fingers curled roughly around Kristan's arm.

"Dusty and Kelsey are dead. So is Billy," Kristan said.

Tommy clenched his jaws. "How?"

"I don't know yet, but it looks as though Davey Robinson was somehow involved. Whoever was with him is also dead."

"And Ashley?"

"I—" Kristan was interrupted by unseen voices. She saw Tina's parents as they ran into the emergency room. There were a number of people running or walking fast into the entryway. Kristan was unsure how many there were although she did recognize Tina's other sister, Carrie, who nodded to Kristan.

"Where's Tina? Where are my grandchildren?" Mary Stickney asked.

As Tommy talked quietly with his mother and father, Kristan stepped outside to the pay telephone. She heard Mary Stickney's gasp as Tommy told her about the children's deaths. Kristan called the Bangor office and asked for her assignment editor. She was relieved when she learned that he had left for the evening.

"Who's night editor?"

"Robin Millerton."

"Tell her I need to talk with her."

"She's on another line," the unseen clerk answered.

"Tell her it's Kristan Cassidy and tell her it's important." Kristan heard the click as she was put on hold.

"Kristan?" Robin's soft voice said. "What's up? You don't usually interrupt me unless it's important."

"Got a bad accident down here, at least four dead. I don't have time to go to my office so I thought I'd dictate what I have." Kristan reached in her back pocket for her reporter's notebook.

"Go," Robin said.

Kristan related the details and the two rewrote the lead several times. "Robin, just say that Ashley is listed in critical condition. I don't know his condition right now, but—" Kristan breathed into the telephone. She could hear Robin's rhythmic tapping on the keyboard.

"Are you all right?" the concerned editor asked.

"I can't answer that," Kristan said, steeling herself. "I know this family. Let's just stick with details."

"You want me to send someone else down to cover this?" Robin asked.

"No," Kristan answered fiercely. "I am the only one who can cover this. I'll call you with an update in about one hour. I know we're pushing deadline, but I—" Kristan inhaled. "May have to if—"

"Regardless if there is an update or not, I want you to call me," Robin said.

"Okay."

Jennifer showed her ID to the young officer. She knew it would be a while before all the police officers knew her on sight. He lifted the yellow police crimescene tape and she ducked underneath.

A slight breeze ruffled her lavender shirt. She saw the chief and several of his officers standing around a bloody young man. The chief looked up as Jennifer approached. He said something quietly to one of his officers and walked toward her.

"Details," Jennifer said.

"Four dead." He nodded toward the mashed gray metal. "A father and his three children were in that."

"Dear God."

"Yeah." Joey's face was stressed to the maximum. "I don't have exact ages yet, but I figure maybe eight or nine. They've been taken to the morgue, along with their father. A third child, probably five or six, was taken to the hospital. I don't know his status yet. Over there—" He nodded toward the tarp in front of the Chevrolet. "One victim, named Jerald McCormick, one of our ne'er-do-wells. The guy standing and bleeding all over himself and everyone else"— Joey's voice hardened—"I think he's the driver. We haven't questioned him yet."

"Badly hurt?"

"Hell no. I'd say the blood is mostly from glass cuts to his forehead and cheeks."

"Take him to the hospital, let the doctors look at him. If he can be interviewed tonight, do it. I want this by the book. Miranda rights. I want witnesses to the interrogation. And tape it," she ordered.

Joey frowned.

"I know, it sounds like I'm telling you your job, chief, but believe me, I'm not. I just want you to make my day in court a little easier," she said gently to him.

Joey did not answer. He nodded toward the Nash. "Impact was unbelievable. It looks as though they hit head-on. I've called in the state police reconstructionist. He just left Bangor, should be here in about two hours. We're finding pieces of that Nash all over the place. There's a headlight over there." Joey nodded at a wooded area a great distance from the road.

"I'm going to look around." She raised a hand. "Don't worry, I'll be careful. I know better than to trample on evidence."

"Well, a lot was trampled even before I got here, but we have enough," Joey said.

"I want you to call me with anything and everything tonight."

"Right." Joey walked back to the officers who stood watching them. "Okay, David, you're going to the hospital."

Jennifer looked at the pile of metal that had once been a Nash. She breathed in deeply. The white seats were splattered with blood. The front of the vehicle was missing. There were two flat tires, no fenders, no trunk lid. Part of the roof had been peeled away. The hood that once covered the engine was in the ditch. She saw a blanket covering something on the ground. She reached down and pulled it back. The dog's glassy eye stared up at her; blood was caked on its mouth. She covered it over again. Jennifer stood up and felt a shudder climb up her spine.

She ran her hand across her mouth and walked to the Chevrolet. At that moment the black hearse had returned and two men were loading the body that had been hidden under the blanket into the back.

Joey and several of his officers were taking David Robinson to one of the cruisers. Joey walked back to her. "I've told two of my fellas to take him to the hospital, we've run out of ambulances. I'll stay until the state cops get here, but when he is ready to be questioned, I'll do it myself."

Jennifer nodded. She studied the angle of the Chevrolet. "Goliath struck David and David lost."

"Yeah. He must have been traveling at a hell of a speed." Joey nodded toward David.

"Look, I'm going to be at my office, so why don't you just come there when you're done."

Jennifer walked away; there was no need for the chief to respond. She knew he would be up most of the night and he would give her a report when he was done.

Just then Kristan pulled up. She said something to the driver and then patted him on the shoulder before the vehicle pulled away. When she saw Jennifer, she said, "I'm sorry about dinner."

Jennifer offered a dismissive wave. She noticed the blood on Kristan's jeans, blood spots on her shirt. "When did you get here?"

"Shortly after it happened." Kristan avoided Jennifer's eyes. "I'm sorry about not calling you, but—" Kristan waved a feeble hand toward the road.

"Kristan, don't worry about dinner." She searched Kristan's face. "You know them." It was a statement, not a question.

Kristan bit hard on her bottom lip. "Yeah." She turned away. "Look, I can't talk about this now, I have to stay—" She paused. "Detached. I've got to get back to the hospital."

Jennifer reached out and touched her arm. "Can I give you a lift to the hospital?"

"Thanks, but I've got my car."

"You want to come over to my office later? I'll be up most of the night waiting for the chief's report," Jennifer said.

"Yeah—no—I don't know. I'll think about that later, okay?" Kristan turned toward her car.

Chapter 14

Kristan headed her car toward Tina's mother's house, but an unexplainable urge pulled her into the city toward Jennifer's office.

She was still numb.

Earlier when she had returned to the emergency room, an armed camp atmosphere gripped even the most casual visitor. David's mother and father had arrived and sat on one side. Kristan surmised that David now was in one of the treatment rooms. Tina's family had formed a tight circle around her on the other side of the waiting area. Tina, with bandages on both hands, looked like a holocaust victim as she stared at the black and white checkered floor.

An occasional cough or the movement of a chair were the only sounds. No one spoke, eyes stared at the not quite yellow walls of the waiting room and the interminable posters about AIDS, Hepatitis B and the evils of smoking.

Hospital staff rushed around in the inner cubicles, and occasionally there was a muffled voice. Except for an occasional telephone ring, there was just the rhythm of silence.

Kristan paced back and forth and was near the nurses' station when she saw Jackie come in and approach Tina. The doctor looked at her and gave a slight shake of her head.

"No," Tina cried out. "No, don't tell me, don't tell me," she pleaded.

Harold pulled his daughter tightly against his chest and Tina's mother and sister began to sob.

Kristan looked over at David Robinson's family and saw his father wipe at his eyes with a tissue. His mother sat stoically staring at her worn tennis shoes.

There were murmurs from Jackie. "I want to see him," Tina begged.

"All right." Jackie left for a moment and then returned, her strong arm circling Tina's shoulder.

Kristan reached over and held Mary's hand. The woman she had known her whole life was barely holding herself together. Harold kept his gaze focused on the floor. Then Tina's cry of pain, the recognition of death. Mary squeezed Kristan's hand and sobbed. Kristan looked at Harold and then looked away from the tears he could no longer control. She stepped back and Harold took his wife in his arms. Tommy, tears on his cheeks, pulled his sister, Carrie, into his arms.

Kristan left Tina's family; it was their moment to grieve alone. She went to the telephone; the story needed an update.

Kristan stopped at the county building. She saw a light in Jennifer's ground-floor office, and she stepped quietly into the entryway. "You should lock your door."

"This is Jefferson County. Nobody locks their door, or so I was told when I moved here. You okay?"

She followed Jennifer into her inner office and dropped into the chair across from the desk. Jennifer sat in the chair next to her.

"Coffee?" She said before Kristan could answer, "Sorry, you don't drink coffee. I have some juice and soft drinks. There are some things in the refrigerator."

"Nothing, thanks. I'm not sure why I'm even here." Kristan's head hurt. She felt ragged, yet angry. "I remember, I am a reporter, and I am here to do my job." Kristan sounded like a mechanical toy. She shifted in her seat. "What are the police charging him with?"

"You know I can't answer that."

"Why not?"

"Because the investigation isn't complete."

"Don't give me that shit. This isn't some minor hit and run, that dirt bag killed five people tonight, three babies." Kristan sprang from the chair and began to pace back and forth. She pushed scraggly hairs off her forehead. She inhaled deeply. "I'm sorry. I want to hit somebody." She stopped to look at Jennifer, who hadn't left her seat.

"Off the record?"

"Yeah. I'm sorry. If I'm going to throw around that I'm here as a reporter, I guess I should start acting like one."

"He denies he was driving. Claims his buddy was, but McCormick is dead. Said he didn't even remember what happened."

Jennifer walked over to the coffeepot on the credenza behind her desk. "They're still questioning him, but he hasn't changed his story." She poured herself a cup of coffee and stirred in cream.

"He's lying."

"Probably."

Kristan shifted into her reporter's mode. "Tomorrow we'll do an in-depth story about the accident, ask people who might have seen the car to call the police. But the reconstructionists should get something."

"Hard to say. The car was pretty badly burned. Looks like it hit the Nash, McCormick was thrown through the window. No seat belts. Robinson got out before it exploded. Fires are bad. My evidence is nothing more than a pile of ashes." Jennifer leaned against the credenza sipping her coffee.

Kristan was trying to control her anger. She used her index finger to emphasize her words. "Someone must have seen him driving before the accident." She stepped closer to Jennifer. "That may be a stretch of barren road, but someone saw him driving. You don't have to worry. This is Jefferson County. People are not afraid to step forward."

"I hope you're right, because I need witnesses who will put him behind the wheel."

"They're out there. My first stop tomorrow will be the chief's office, then I'll come over here. I know you can't say much, but you can say you are looking for eyewitnesses."

"Kristan, I'm sorry. Was she a friend?"

Kristan, her hand on the door, said, "Yeah, a good friend." She quietly closed the door behind her.

Chapter 15

Kristan looked at her watch. She had fifteen minutes. What the heck, she was supposed to meet Jennifer at Tippys, but she decided it would be nicer to walk over with her. It was a perfect Down East day, and only two days before the start of June. The streets and stores were starting to fill up with tourists. The temperature was around 70, and there was a gentle breeze coming off the water. She locked her office door and zipped across the road to Jennifer's office.

Brenda was just leaving. "Hey, lady."

"Kristan." Brenda gave her a motherly hug. "You okay?" Concern filled her eyes.

"Just okay."

"How's Tina?"

"Not good. She's withdrawn. Won't even talk to me. The days have been a nightmare. Tina's family is afraid to leave her alone. She just sits and looks at the television screen. I don't think she sees anything."

"I went to the funeral." Brenda visibly shuddered. "Those tiny little coffins. No one should have to go through that," she said angrily. "No one." Kristan knew Brenda was thinking of her own daughter.

"I know. The word *tragedy* is meaningless. It isn't a big enough word to describe what happened. Tina has stopped talking to everyone, and she's ignored suggestions of counseling. She even refused to talk with her minister."

Brenda looked up as Jennifer closed the door behind her. "Ah, here's your date?"

Kristan shifted her eyes from Brenda to Jennifer and blushed. Jennifer laughed.

"I'll see you after lunch," Brenda said as she turned toward her car.

"I thought it might be nice to walk to Tippys." Kristan felt she needed to fill the space and ignore Brenda's remark.

"I'd like that. Can I set some ground rules?"

"Sure."

"Let's talk about anything but the accident. That is all I have focused on since the crash, and I would just love to think about something else for about an hour."

"Agreed." They walked along companionably. "How do you feel about history?"

"Very impartial." Jennifer grinned. "What kind of history?"

"Well, right here. See that?" Kristan stopped in front of what was known as the Chester Dean house, a large three-story captain's house with a widow's walk, set back from the bay. A nearly nine-acre perfectly mowed lawn reached down to the shore. "During the War of Eighteen Twelve," Kristan said, pointing to the bay, "the redcoats rowed their longboats across Johnson's Bay right to this shore."

"You are making this up."

"No, really." Kristan resumed the stroll toward Tippys. Jennifer fell in step with her. "They got out of their longboats and in typical British fashion marched in military formation up to this very road." She interrupted her story to hold the door open for Jennifer. Kristan waved to several of the locals as she led Jennifer to one of the tables at the back of the diner. "What the British didn't know is that the locals had gotten wind of the planned invasion and were hiding with their guns inside the few stores on Front Street, on top of roofs of houses and behind trees. The minute the British hit the road—" Kristan stopped as Theresa walked over.

"Want menus or you going for the usual?" she asked Kristan.

"What's the usual?" Jennifer asked.

"For her, fish and chips."

"That sounds good to me. I don't need a menu. Besides, I want to hear the rest of this story."

"Two usuals," Kristan said. "Anyway, the men opened fire right at this column of soldiers. Several were killed, others wounded. When the smoke cleared the British threw down their guns, picked up their wounded and headed back to the Dean house. Inside, Mrs. Dean, who had been a midwife, patched up the wounded as best she could, as they say around here, and the British loaded them into their long-boats rowed back to Bayshore, and that was the local battle of Eighteen Twelve."

"Now, I know you're putting me on. Why would the locals, as you call them, allow them to escape?"

"No jail to keep them in, and they figured they'd never be back once they got their butts kicked."

Jennifer laughed. "I love that story. Got any more?"

"Zillions."

"I want to hear all of them."

"That would take a lifetime." Kristan stopped, knowing that was a leading statement.

"I've got a lifetime," Jennifer offered quietly, again with the unwavering stare.

Kristan couldn't look away from those brown eyes. She felt her heart do a two-step. She ran her tongue across her dry lips.

"Two usuals." Theresa put the plates in front of them. "Extra tartar. Coffee for you." She nodded at Jennifer. "And milk for you." Theresa picked up her tray and hesitated. "Kristan, I was real sorry about Tina. I know she's a friend. I couldn't imagine facing the next day if that happened to my family."

"Thanks." Kristan didn't know how to fill the awkward silence.

"Well, if you need something, just holler."

Jennifer cut the steaming fried fish with her fork. "How long have you known Tina?"

"She's younger than I am, but we grew up together. Her family lived just down the road from where I grew up. I even baby-sat her a few times. Not a lot because mostly families did that for each other. Then I went away to college, and we went our separate ways. She married Billy and . . . let me think." Kristan scratched the back of her head. "She had the twins, then after I got back she had Ashley. I don't know. We just reconnected after that."

"I heard she's not doing too well."

"No, she's not. I'm worried. Something was going on in her life before the accident and now she has just shut down. I feel so helpless."

"What do you mean?"

"Well," Kristan said as she dabbed a French fry in some ketchup, "the evening you and I were going to have dinner, she called me. Said she had something important to talk about. I had helped her get a job as an aide at the elementary school, and I thought she just wanted to talk about that, possibly that Billy didn't want her to work."

"And?"

"I don't know, my instinct tells me there was something more serious going on and she needed to talk about it." Kristan dropped the uneaten French fry and rested her thumb against her lips.

"You feel guilty that you didn't talk with her?"

"It wouldn't have changed history. The accident still would have happened, but maybe it would have helped penetrate this fortress she's climbed into. I don't know."

"Have you tried to talk with her?"

"Yeah, many times. She won't talk. Not just to me, to anyone."

"That's tough and the sad part is you can't force her to get professional help if she doesn't want it."

"Yeah. Look we said we wouldn't talk about anything having to do with the accident and here we are doing that. Let's shift focus."

"Agreed. You can help me."

"How?"

"Well, I'm planing to renovate my grandmother's house. Tear out a few walls, replace electrical wiring, chimney. Minor alterations," Jennifer said with mock seriousness.

"Ah. Do you plan on living somewhere else while you have all of these minor alterations done?"

"Naw, we Ogdens are tough. I'll live there."

"Jennifer, I did some minor alterations, as you call them, to my house when I first bought it. Believe me, it is a mess. You are going to find you have dust and dirt everywhere. For months I lived in two rooms. Half of my furniture was stacked in the kitchen. The other half was in my bedroom. I had one chair to sit in and had to run the gauntlet to get to my bed. If you can, live somewhere else until the work is finished."

"Well, first of all, I don't have another place, and second, I think it would be fun to watch the metamorphosis. Anyway, I brought it up because I'm looking for some good carpenters, plumbers, electricians."

"We have some good ones." Kristan nodded as Theresa returned with the checks.

"Can I get you anything else?" Theresa turned to Jennifer. "Dessert?"

"I'd love it, but the fish filled me up. Maybe next time."

Kristan slid from the booth and stood up. She wanted to reach out and help Jennifer but instead pushed her hands deep into her pockets.

"Anyway." Jennifer picked up the thread of their conversation on the way back to their offices. "Have any recommendations?"

"Sure, there are several good people around. There's a woman I heard about. There also are several good male carpenters."

"Well, I'd prefer a woman. Do you have her name?"

"It's Jean something. I don't know her myself, but I can call you later with the information." They were standing outside Jennifer's office.

"I'd like that."

Kristan felt her shy shield closing in around her.

"I've enjoyed this. Thanks for asking me to lunch. I'd like to do this again."

Kristan grinned. "Me too. And we will, I promise."

"Well, call me with that information." Jennifer smiled and turned to her door. Kristan turned to go to her office. "Maybe we could have dinner sometime."

"I'd like that," Kristan said. Kristan restrained herself from doing a dance as she crossed the road.

Chapter 16

Kristan looked at the court calendar. There was a motion for a new trial on an attempted shooting that she worked on last year. She was still worried about the case involving Billy and the kids. She'd talked with the police a lot after the accident and Robinson continued to deny that he was driving.

The only thing Kristan believed she had accomplished was that the news story she had written the day after the accident had motivated several people who had seen Robinson driving a halfhour before the accident to come forward.

He was arraigned within days of the accident and charged with five counts of vehicular manslaughter, five counts of operating a motor vehicle while under the influence of intoxicants, as well as one count of reckless conduct with a dangerous weapon, his vehicle. The trial was scheduled for August.

As she sat at her computer, Kristan tried to focus on a news story about a new paper process at the mill. The cool spring weather of

April and May had given way to a warmer June, and Kristan was looking forward to fall. Memorial Day had been a blur of work and worry about Tina. The funeral had evoked raw emotions. Not even Francis could keep from crying. A month later, Kristan's eyes still blurred with tears each time she thought about the three tiny coffins.

She and Jennifer had met for lunch several times since the accident, and she found herself enjoying this newfound affinity. Many times she had resisted the urge to call Jennifer or go over to her office. Jennifer was bright and fun to be with. The few times she had to go talk about a case, she felt Brenda's unspoken smile.

The ringing telephone returned her to the present.

"Kristan, Joey."

"Hey, chief. What's happening?"

"I need to talk with you off the record."

"Go for it."

"I've heard that the new A.D.A. wants to plead the case." Joey didn't have to say which case. Kristan had heard the rumors.

She dropped her feet off her desk and sat forward. "I've heard that, but I didn't believe it."

"Believe it. Robinson's attorney claims that even though people saw him driving prior to the accident, he switched with McCormick just minutes before the accident."

"That's a lie," Kristan said disgustedly. She felt her stomach tighten. "I heard he had just bought the car. He was driving, and you and I know it."

"Yeah, but there were no eyewitnesses at the time of impact, or at least no one has come forward. You know, that's a pretty lonely stretch of road, no houses."

"Is there a case without eyewitnesses?"

"Pretty circumstantial. I think she can win, but she needs to go to court."

"Joey, if she agrees to a plea bargain, she'll be run out of town."

"I think she's afraid they'll run her out of town if she loses."

"Have you spoken with Francis?"

"I think he's the one pushing for the plea bargain. He's lost his fight."

"Have you spoken with her?"

"Yes, but—"

"But?"

"I thought maybe you could talk with her."

"Jeez, Joey, that is so far out of my frame of reference. You know I'm supposed to be uninvolved."

"Hey, kid, this is Joey you're talking to. I know the times when you've worked in the background to influence the outcome of things. Besides, I hear you two are friends."

Kristan frowned. Damn small town, she thought. "I'll talk to her," she told Joey, "but no promises."

"I think she just needs someone not involved in the court system to argue from a different perspective."

"I'll try, but if she refuses to talk about it, I'm not going to push."

"I owe you a big one on this, Kristan."

"You bet, big time."

Kristan immediately dialed Jennifer's number.

Brenda answered. "I want you to take the rest of the day off with double pay," Kristan joked without any preliminary introduction.

"Great. Bye. I'm gone," Brenda responded.

"Whoa. You can't leave until you help me, then you can take the rest of the day off with double pay."

"I knew there'd be a catch."

"How's the daughter?" Kristan knew that Brenda's only daughter was headed for college in a few months. "Is Mom going to get all teary-eyed?"

"No, Mom isn't." Brenda laughed. "Mom is going to be relieved, but Dad might cry. You'd think we were shipping her off to Timbuktu." She exaggerated the last word. "She's anxious to get going. You looking for Jennifer?"

"How'd you know? I could have been looking for Francis."

Brenda chuckled.

"Is she in?" Kristan frowned at the telephone. She did not want to pursue any further how Brenda might have known.

"Yup. Hold the line."

"Hi." Jennifer's voice was soft. Kristan's heart skipped a beat.

"I was wondering if you'd like to grab a bite to eat. Talk."

"When?"

"Tonight. That is, if you don't have any plans," Kristan offered hastily.

"Another golden arches special?"

"No." Kristan laughed. "I thought maybe Shoreside, someplace nice. My treat."

"How about my place? This morning I felt very ambitious and started a crockpot of beef stew."

"I wasn't looking for—"

"I know, but it seems sad to waste it. Plus, I have a feeling you want to talk about the Robinson case, and I don't want to do it in public."

Kristan hesitated. "You are one bright lady. How'd you know?"

"Because that's what everyone wants to talk about right now. Kristan, I know you are a woman of considerable charm." Kristan could hear the mirth in Jennifer's voice. "But we are going to do what is right to get him behind bars, including a possible plea bargain, so this could be a wasted conversation."

"Could be, but I'm willing to gamble. What time?"

"I should be out of here by six. How about seven?"

"Sounds great. What can I bring?"

"Same as the last time, nothing."

Kristan's mind did a playback—the rush to the accident and then the hospital.

"Let's keep the murder and mayhem to zero tonight, okay?" Jennifer said softly.

Kristan chuckled. "Okay, see you tonight, and I promise if there is a news crisis I'll ignore it."

"Right," Jennifer said skeptically. "See you tonight."

Chapter 17

Kristan knew that fussing over what she was going to wear to Jennifer's was tantamount to focusing on the visit as a date rather than as a meeting. She tucked her dark blue blouse into her jeans and put on her black suede vest. She grabbed the bottle of chilled Beringer's white zinfandel and ran out the door. She left the ringing telephone behind. Not tonight, she thought.

As she pulled into Jennifer's driveway, she breathed a sigh of relief. No accidents, no murder, no mayhem.

"Welcome." Jennifer stepped back from the door with an exaggerated sweep of her arm culminating in a slight bow. She had a mischievous grin on her face. "I expected the telephone to ring any minute."

"For you," Kristan said as she held out the bottle of wine. She followed Jennifer into the kitchen. "It smells good in here." But it wasn't only the beef stew that made Kristan's mouth water.

Standing next to Jennifer, Kristan decided there was something absolutely beguiling about her. It wasn't beauty or her sexuality; it was her selfassurance.

"I hope it's good. I make it all the time but never the same. It depends on what I have in the house." Jennifer looked quizzically at Kristan. "Come on." She reached for Kristan's arm.

Kristan swallowed hard as she felt the warm hand through her sleeve. She wondered if that was what being branded felt like. Cool down, lady, Kristan told herself. You are here for an important discussion. Keep your head out of the bed. "Busy day?" she asked.

"Somewhat. Discussion first or dinner?"

Kristan grinned. "You're direct, counselor. Discussion. Let's get business behind us."

"Okay. Wine?"

Kristan nodded yes.

She waved Kristan into the living room. "I'll join you in a second."

Kristan walked around the room. She looked at the pictures of Jennifer with, Kristan assumed, her mother and father, and Jennifer alone. But no pictures of the girlfriend.

Jennifer came back into the room and handed her a glass of wine. She sat on the couch and curled her right leg under her.

In spite of her resolve, Kristan stared at the curled leg, the bared toes. The arch of her foot took on a sensuous edge. Kristan swallowed and stood clutching the wineglass.

"I heard today that you might plead the Robinson case." Kristan shook her head; her mode of address was too formal. She sat down in a chair and put her wine down. "Any truth to that rumor?"

"It's not a rumor. Francis and I are entertaining an offer from Robinson's attorney. He pleads to two of the manslaughter charges and agrees to do a minimum of five years in prison." Jennifer frowned. "I assume we are talking off the record here."

Kristan made a curt, dismissive gesture. "Of course. I wouldn't be here otherwise."

"It's not a bad offer."

"Right, a year for each dead person." Kristan was on edge.

"No. Not one year for each dead person," Jennifer said. Kristan sensed the deep stirring of anger in her. "A guarantee of prison. We go to trial, we have a guarantee of nothing."

"You can't plead this case."

"Oh, and why not?"

Kristan sighed in resignation. "People will be outraged."

"And if we lose?"

"People will be outraged."

Jennifer raised her eyebrow.

"But the difference is, people will feel you tried."

"Well, trying is not good enough. I know he was driving. We don't have much else. There were beer cans in the car and he was drunk. Blood level right at the point-zero-eight level. Drunk, but not blotto."

"The other intoxicant, pot?"

"Yup. I feel we can show he was hopped up on marijuana prior to the accident. We found traces of THC Delta Nine in his blood. It's a byproduct of marijuana. It's a complicated formula, but we were able to tell how much he had in his blood even a half-hour before the accident. We also can show minor traces of downers, but no high numbers," Jennifer added.

"Then prove it. Go to trial," Kristan said in exasperation.

"Kristan." Jennifer pushed her hair back from her forehead in a gesture that betrayed her frustration. Her voice was purposeful. "Let me say this in tiny little words." She leaned forward, using her hands to emphasize each word. "We have Robinson behind the wheel one half-hour before the accident, but no one saw him driving just before the collision. He's adamant that he wasn't driving, and we can't prove otherwise. According to him, his buddy was driving."

"Then why the plea? If he's not guilty I would think he would want this to go to trial."

Jennifer sighed. "Doesn't want to gamble. Feels the case is so emotional, he can't get a fair trial."

"He wants to plead because he's guilty. David Robinson never would turn the wheel over to Jerald McCormick. He was too much of a control freak. Driving made the twit feel macho."

"Macho attitude doesn't get it. I need proof. Otherwise he will walk."

"You might not be able to put him behind the wheel seconds before the accident, but you can put him there every other time he drove. There is a pattern to his behavior."

"I am not going to convict him on a pattern." Jennifer stood up. "It's too circumstantial. Look, I'm not even sure why I'm discussing this with you. This is Francis's call. He wants me to plead, we plead."

"Francis is old and tired, and I know damn well that if you tell him you want to go to trial, he'll do it. The impediment here is you, not Francis."

Jennifer's eyes sparked. "And you have no objectivity when it comes to this case."

Kristan bit hard on the inside of her cheek. "I am objective enough to know when you are wimping out of a trial."

"Wimping out. How dare you. You try putting a case of this magnitude together, with this much public emotion, and tell me I am wimping out. I'll tell you who's wimping out: you. All you have to do is stand back and criticize everyone else. Well, I am a player in this. I have to pull it together, and my goal is to get him in prison. If that means plea bargaining, than by golly I am going to do it."

"You're a coward."

Jennifer's face was flushed. "I have never thrown anyone out of my house," Jennifer said between clenched teeth. "But—"

Kristan held up her hands, and they served as the punctuation mark to the end of Jennifer's sentence. "I'm going." She turned and stalked off, leaving Jennifer standing in the middle of the room.

❧

Kristan still was smoldering when she got home. She punched in Jackie's number.

"You're home early. How was the date?"

"There was no date." Kristan was vexed.

"Uh-oh. I haven't heard you sound this angry in a long time."

"The woman is impossible."

"And you're not? So tell me what happened."

It took Kristan only minutes to relate the conversation. "And then I stormed out."

"Very mature. She's right, you have no objectivity in this, because of Tina and . . ." Jackie paused.

Although she was fuming inside, she knew better than to hang up on Jackie. That had happened once before when they had a fight, and Jackie hadn't spoken to her for days. After that fight they had talked about Kristan's inability to confront people when she was angry. Jackie refused to allow Kristan to blame it on the times she ran away from her father's anger.

"Kristan, your anger is way out of proportion to what's going on. I agree with Jennifer. Tina is your friend, so who's arguing for the trial, Kristan the reporter or Kristan the friend? Maybe you need to step back from this and get another reporter to cover it. The D.A.'s office agrees to plea bargains all the time."

"Jacks, I know neither you nor Jennifer believe this, but it has to go to trial. I'm not saying this because Tina is a friend. People here are really upset. More so than with any other accident I can remember. Even people who don't know Tina are angry, because it could have been them on that road. I'm arguing for closure. It would be a catharsis, Jacks. People here need a trial to have that catharsis. Not just Tina and her family but everyone."

Jackie said, "Why don't you tell that to Jennifer? That's a pretty convincing argument."

"I can't because I stupidly lost my temper and stormed out."

"Call her."

"Aw, I don't think I could do that. What if she hangs up?"

"Then she hangs up. Call her, Kristan. Tell her what you told me." Kristan did not respond. "You know, you are one of the most confrontational reporters I've ever met, but it amazes me how hard it is for you to confront someone when it becomes personal."

"Okay, okay, doc. No more psychoanalysis." Kristan glanced at the clock. It was still early. "I'll call her."

"Start by apologizing."

"Apologizing? Why? She's the one who threatened to throw me out of her house."

"Apologize."

"All right," Kristan grumbled. "But I hope you're proud of yourself. I just love eating crow," Kristan said sarcastically.

"It'll do you some good. Humble you."

"I have enough humble to make a pie. Thanks, Jacks." Kristan hung up and punched up Jennifer's home number. The telephone rang several times. "Come on, I know you're there. Answer," Kristan mumbled.

"Hello."

"Hi, it's me." Kristan rushed on past the silence. "Look, I apologize. I said some pretty unpleasant things, and I was wrong." She paused.

"Well, I said some pretty unpleasant things too and I'm sorry."

"Can we start over?"

"You mean dinner?"

"Well, it might be too late for that, but . . ."

"No, it's not. The baking powder biscuits are like rocks, but the stew is pretty good. Come on. I'll set another place." Jennifer chuckled, diffusing some of the tension. "I yanked your plate off the table after you left. You have a wonderful dinner-party repartee. Do you do things like that often?"

"It probably explains why I don't get asked out very much." Kristan joined in the kidding.

"So, you want to start again?"

"I'll be right over. The liquor store is closed, so we'll have to do with the bottle of wine I brought earlier."

"Kristan, before we get into the heavy stuff, let's just talk. It might be nice to get to know each other."

"Agreed."

The first few minutes were awkward, but they had agreed to a truce and small talk. They laughed and shared college stories over stew and wine. Then they compared job battle notes.

"That was delicious." Kristan sat back.

"Thank you." Jennifer smiled impishly, and Kristan hoped she was enjoying her company.

"Let me help you with dishes."

Jennifer rose. "I'll let you, but you have to promise that if we start arguing again, you won't hit the hostess over the head with her own dishes."

"Promise." Kristan held up her hands in open surrender. "Where's the dish pan?"

"Under the sink." Jennifer busied herself with clearing the table. "You're serious? You want to wash them?"

Kristan held her hands under the warm water then poured soap into the pan. "I am quite an accomplished dishwasher. If there ever was a category called dishwashing in the Olympics, I can assure you I would score a perfect ten."

"Humble thing, aren't you." Jennifer stood next to Kristan as she dumped several dishes into the soapy water.

"I've been told I need more of that."

"More of what?"

"Humble."

Jennifer turned and grinned and Kristan was drawn to Jennifer's dark liquid eyes. She kept her hands buried in the soap, fearing she would reach across, soapy hands and all, and pull Jennifer into a kiss. She knew what was stopping her. The image of Pam touching Jennifer's cheek flashed like a comet; it was burned into her memory.

"Uh, Jennifer?" Kristan stared down at the soapy suds. "I want to try an argument on you." She glanced sideways, trying to gauge Jennifer's expression. "An argument of linear reasoning."

"Okay." Jennifer stopped what she was doing. Her brown eyes were intent.

Kristan talked at length about the accident and the impact it had on the community. "If ever there was something called a unifying anger, this is it. Try the case, so people can diffuse that anger. They can only do it if they live through each day of a trial. Anything else, and they are going to feel cheated."

Jennifer was studiously quiet. "I can buy that. But what happens if the judge, or possibly a jury, lets him walk. Does the anger come back, maybe never go away?"

"I don't know, but I think you have to take that chance." Kristan washed the last pan and dumped out the water, then turned to Jennifer. "Just think about it, okay?"

"Okay." Jennifer stood just inches from her, the dish towel still in her hand.

Kristan swallowed. She glanced up at the clock. "I've got an early appointment." She felt flustered.

Jennifer stepped back. "Me too."

They said nothing as they walked to the door. Jennifer kissed Kristan on the cheek. "Thanks. I'll talk about this with Francis. I promise."

Kristan shoved her hands in her pockets. "I really had a good time tonight."

"Me too."

Kristan walked to her car. Every nerve in her body was singing as she put the key in the ignition. She hesitated before starting the engine but resisted the urge to go back inside. Great, she thought. First you storm out, now you want to storm back. This wasn't going to work. She felt like an awkward adolescent. All the years of celibacy seemed to hang like a block and tackle around her neck. You got it bad, kiddo, she said to herself as she put the car in gear. Real bad.

Chapter 18

Kristan nodded to several people as she entered Superior Court. Although she was the first reporter to arrive, she knew the high-profile case would drag in television talking heads from as far away as Bangor. She was pleased when Toby and Marcy finally arrived.

"Going to be a hell of a case," Toby said quietly.

"Yeah."

Marcy searched Kristan's face. "How's Tina doing?"

"Barely holding it together, but she is going to be here. Her mother told me she'd be here every day of the trial."

"I couldn't." Marcy shook her head and looked as Tina, surrounded by family members, walked into the courtroom.

Francis and Jennifer were seated at the prosecutor's table. Jennifer looked in Kristan's direction and smiled.

Kristan's heart did a two-step, but she stomped on the emotion. Jennifer still had someone in her life. She watched Jennifer out of the corner of her eye as she went to the railing that separated the public from the legal proceedings to speak with Tina and her family. At that moment, Jennifer took Tina's hand in both of hers. Kristan could not hear the words, but she saw the look in Tina's eyes. Jennifer had become her lifeline to reality. Kristan sensed their connection. It was not unrealistic, because she knew that when Francis had a particularly difficult case, he would connect with the victims to let them know that something was being done.

David Robinson and his attorney were seated at the defense table. The attorney, Thomas Heater, was an import from Portland, and Kristan did not know him. Robinson kept looking around the courtroom for support, and his face lit up as his mother, father and three sisters entered the courtroom. He nodded to them.

The sharp rap on the judge's chamber door directed everyone's attention to the front of the court. "All rise," the bailiff ordered. "Judge Margaret McDermott presiding."

"She any good?" Toby whispered to Kristan.

"Don't know. This is the first time I've seen her," Kristan whispered back.

The first issue before the court was Robinson's decision to waive a jury trial.

Good move by the defense, Kristan thought. She had seen the accident scene photos and knew they would sway a jury.

The judge discussed the decision with Robinson at length to make certain he understood what he was giving up. Robinson mumbled yes to each of the judge's questions. The judge was no-nonsense. Assured that he understood the rules, she told Jennifer to begin her opening argument.

Jennifer described the events that led up to the fatal accident. She said evidence would prove that Robinson was driving the Chevrolet that collided with the Nash, and the results of urine tests taken after the crash would show that Robinson had a combination of alcohol, marijuana and downers in his system at the time. The evidence, she said, also would prove that excessive speed was a factor.

117

Kristan watched as the television reporters scribbled furiously in their pads. She knew the details, so except for a quotation here and there, she could pay more attention to Jennifer's delivery than to her words. She liked the A.D.A.'s soft-spoken style, her eye contact with the judge.

When Jennifer finished her opening statement, she sat down. Kristan smiled as Jennifer took a deep breath and held it. She was, no doubt, getting a hold on the butterflies in her stomach.

The judge nodded to Robinson's attorney, Thomas Heater. Kristan sat up as Heater began. He paced and pointed. He was a fiery contrast to Jennifer's low-key manner. He said the sequence of events demonstrated that a tragic accident had occurred, but he argued that his client was not driving and had not confessed to driving the vehicle those last few fatal seconds before the crash. He pointed out that all three adults—Robinson, McCormick and Billy Randall—had drunk alcohol before the crash. He said he believed the case should be dealt with by a civil rather than a criminal court.

Kristan held her breath this time. She looked over at Tina and her family. She knew that on the day of the crash, Billy had been at a friend's house working on a car. David had stopped by and the three had shared a six-pack. Then Billy left. Tina stared hard at the attorney, but there was no flicker of acknowledgment that she may have known about the alcohol.

The first witness called to the stand was Tina's mother. Jennifer handed her school photographs of each of her grandchildren and asked her to identify them. Mary choked back the tears. She hesitated as she looked at each photograph, and her voice broke when she came to the picture of her five-year-old grandson, Ashley. Jennifer then handed the pictures to the judge. These pictures would contrast sharply with those taken by police at the scene. Kristan knew that the impression of three happy smiling children now was imprinted in the judge's memory.

When Robinson's attorney said he had no questions of Mary, Jennifer called Jake Stanley to the stand. Stanley had seen Robinson driving the car about 20 minutes before the crash. He said he and his wife were traveling toward Bailey's Cove when the black Chevrolet passed them at a high rate of speed. He said he knew David Robinson. "Had known 'the boy' all his life."

Kristan cringed. Robinson was thirty years old. When did boys become men?

Sean McLadden, who worked for Spark's Ambulance, was the first medical person to arrive at the scene. He spoke directly to the judge as he described the scene. "I saw the Chevrolet first, or a car, it was a ball of fire. David Robinson was standing in front of the vehicle. There was a person lying on the ground. I knew him to be Jerald McCormick. I checked him for vitals, nothing. I was going to check Robinson when I heard cries coming from the other vehicle." Sean paused. "Well, it didn't look like a car. It was this huge twist of metal. I was afraid of another fire. I went over and that was when I saw a body on the ground. I checked for vitals—no pulse," he said of Billy Randall. "I looked into the car and saw a young boy trapped on the passenger's side, in the backseat. He was awake, breathing, screaming, more like a scream-type moan. A second child, a girl who later I learned was Kelsey Randall, was next to the car. The impact had ripped the seat from its mooring, and she was thrown, still strapped in the seatbelt."

"What did you see next?" Jennifer's voice sounded as though it was coming from a faraway place.

Kristan held her breath.

"I looked across to the other passenger in the backseat of the vehicle. I saw the boy and recognized immediately that he was deceased."

"How did you know?" Jennifer asked.

"He was decapitated." Sean's voice was barely above a whisper.

Kristan heard the gasps. Tina, her hands pressed tightly against her mouth, sobbed.

Jennifer waited, then quietly said, "No more questions."

The judge looked at Robinson's attorney. "No questions," Heater said.

After a long pause while Jennifer looked at her notes, she called her next witness. A chain of medical personnel, including Jackie, testified about their pieces of the puzzle to help recreate the scene for the judge.

Jackie was the consummate professional as she answered Jennifer's questions about the accident. Kristan was proud of her friend. Here was a woman she truly loved, someone she would want by her side if she was ever hurt or hurting.

Jackie replayed in words everything Kristan had seen at the accident—the rush to help first Kelsey and then Billy, then the effort to help Ashley. Kristan shivered. She wondered if the memory of those bloody moments, those painful cries from Ashley, would ever leave her.

Kristan was not surprised when Robinson's attorney had no questions for Jackie.

Paul Sparks, who owned the ambulance service, also testified. He said he drove the ambulance that took Ashley to the hospital and that it was obvious that the child was seriously injured.

"How did you know?" Jennifer asked.

"There was a lot of internal bleeding."

Sparks said that while he was in the emergency room he heard a loud male voice arguing with a nurse and he went to see if the nurse needed help. "He called the nurse a fucking bitch and said she was hurting him."

"Did you know the man?"

"Oh, yes, I know David Robinson well. We went to school together."

"Did Robinson say anything else?"

"Not really, but the nurse did ask him a question."

"What question?"

Kristan could feel the tension increase as spectators watched and listened.

"She asked him if he had been driving."

"What did David say?"

"He just stared at her."

"I object." David's attorney was on his feet. "He is not trained to read nonverbal communication."

The judge turned to Jennifer. "This man was in the examining room. He is testifying to what he saw," Jennifer said quietly.

"Overruled."

Kristan felt drained, and she could imagine how Jennifer felt. The hours of testimony had been riveting. She was relieved when the judge, who seemed to be the only one in the courtroom to have a handle on the time, said they would break for lunch.

Kristan nodded to the two other reporters. "I'm going to the office. I have an hour to write at least this morning's summary."

"Me too, I can have it on the air in an hour," Toby agreed.

"You okay?" Kristan said to Marcy, who had not moved.

"You saw him."

Kristan averted her eyes.

"You saw that little boy." Marcy persisted, "Decapitated?"

"Yes."

"They should hang the bastard," Marcy said fiercely.

"Whoa, lady. He hasn't been found guilty yet," Toby said gently.

"He's guilty," Marcy hissed. "God, poor Tina. Did she know?"

"I don't think the D.A. told her." Kristan looked in Tina's direction. Their eyes locked, then a curtain dropped over Tina's expression and she turned away.

"Why?"

"Who could?" Kristan asked the question more in the air than of Marcy. "Look, I've got to go. I'm going to be pushing deadline if I don't write at least this half of the trial now." When she left, Marcy still was sputtering.

Kristan looked over at Jennifer and found her watching her. Kristan gave her a thumbs up, then turned away and hurried out of the courtroom. Her exchange with Marcy had cost her five minutes, and she needed another five minutes to get to her office and her computer.

Kristan's fingers flew across the keyboard as she recorded the details of the morning trial. Before she knew it, the clock told her she only had a few minutes to get back to the courthouse.

She ran across the road, through the wooden doors and up the stairs. She paused to catch her breath outside the dark oak doors that separated her from the courtroom, then went in. Sergeant Robert Beam of the Maine State Police already was on the stand. He was the state's reconstructionist, so she was pretty sure where the testimony would go.

As she sat down next to Marcy and Toby she whispered, "Did I miss much?"

"Not really, it just started," Marcy whispered back.

Kristan settled in; it would be an afternoon of technical witnesses.

Kristan watched as the judge eyed the clock. It was four-thirty and the attorneys looked drained. The chief of police had been on the stand most of the afternoon detailing his investigation. Kristan sighed relief when Heater said he had no more questions.

"If you both are through with this witness"—the judge looked from Jennifer to Heater—"then I suggest because of the lateness of the hour that we adjourn until eight a.m. tomorrow."

"All rise," the bailiff said.

Kristan stuck her reporter's notebook in her back pocket. "Gotta go, guys, see you tomorrow," she said to Marcy and Toby.

"Hey, want to grab supper tonight?" Toby asked her.

"Can't. Don't know what's been going on at my office all day. I may have extra stories to cover before this night's done."

"Cool."

Kristan sat in front of her computer screen. The story had been in Bangor for an hour, and there were no calls from her assignment editor. She opened her mail and replayed the messages on her answering machine. Nothing so shattering that it couldn't wait until after the trial, she decided.

She glanced at her watch. Seven p.m. She picked up the telephone and dialed. The four rings told her Jennifer was not in or not answering, and the machine came on.

"Hi, Jennifer. This is Kristan. Just—" Kristan heard the click.

"Don't hang up," Jennifer said. "Hang on while I figure out how to turn this damn thing off." There was another click.

"Just called to reprise a Down East expression. Ya done good today."

"Thanks. But I still haven't put him in the driver's seat."

"You will."

"I wish I had your confidence. Tomorrow, I have witnesses that were with them when David was driving, witnesses who saw him driving that day, but no silver bullet."

"You won't need a silver bullet. Your case is good, Jennifer."

"Let's hope. Kristan, thanks for the call."

Kristan paused a long time, her mind racing. She had so many questions she wanted to ask, but not now. Finally she said, "I'm glad I called. First because I'm the one who pushed for the trial, and I really wanted you to know I thought it was going well and now because—well."

"I'm glad you called too. See you in court." Jennifer chuckled.

"Definitely."

Jennifer was relieved when she hung up the telephone. Pam had been calling twice a day and she sensed a desperation in her. She was able to plead the pressures of preparation for the trial and the trial as an excuse for keeping Pam in Portland. She had too much to think about, and right now it didn't include her relationship with Pam.

Chapter 19

By the third day of the trial, everyone connected with it was over-wrought, including the usually steady Francis. He was not carrying the weight of the case, but every day he was in the second chair handing Jennifer notes and whispering in her ear. Kristan could tell he was feeling the stress, because when they met in the hallway before or after court, he didn't offer the usual down-home story or quip. All she got was a nod.

Jennifer had sequestered herself in the law library. Kristan was sure the Bangor television crews wouldn't show up, because the trial had bogged down into more technical evidence. Lacking any photo opportunities, they had to look elsewhere for gore.

Kristan looked up as Toby rushed into the courtroom with five minutes to spare. "I hate early mornings," he complained.

"Not my bag either."

"What's on for today?"

"Why do you think I would know that?"

Toby chuckled.

"All right, the state plans to call a forensic toxicologist and chemist. I expect it's going to get fairly technical. They'll talk about what kinds of drugs and how much alcohol Robinson had in his system."

Toby groaned. "I think I should have stayed home."

Later, after a day of boring and repetitive testimony, Kristan rushed back to her office to write her story. Jennifer had scored points. Her expert witnesses said that the only person under the influence of drugs and alcohol at the time of the crash was Robinson. Heater had been unable to shake their testimony.

It was five p.m. and she was ready to head home. She had been relieved when the judge decided to quit at three. Today's account of the trial was short. Too much technical stuff buried the reader, and although she had digested a great deal of information, what she included was minimal, just enough to give a flavor of the day's courtroom events.

She had an urge to call Jennifer, but resisted. She decided to call Jackie instead.

"How goes the trial?" Jackie asked after they had waltzed through the preliminaries.

"Good, I think. You want to go get a bite?"

"Sure, I'll be at the office for another hour, but I could meet you somewhere."

"Let's go upscale. I don't feel like fried-food heaven tonight."

"Shoreside's, say, at six?" Jackie asked, and Kristan agreed.

She was seated at the bar when Jackie arrived.

"Hey, little buddy, I've been following your stories," Jackie said as she settled on the stool next to Kristan. "What's left?"

"I suspect the state will rest tomorrow. That will give Heater the weekend. He'll begin his case Monday."

"Who's winning?"

Kristan signaled the bartender. She ordered a white zinfandel for herself and a Sea Dog, a beer from one of Maine's microbreweries, for Jackie. "Hard to tell. Sometimes Jennifer scores, then Heater slips in a few." Kristan pushed her hair off her forehead. "People ask me that question a lot, but you really can't tell until all the information is in place. It's like a giant puzzle—the dynamics of the picture change with each new piece."

"Apt analogy."

Kristan looked past Jackie to see Jim Stevenson's slight wave. "I think our table is ready."

Jackie waited until they were seated, had their menus and had learned about the specials before she asked Kristan about Jennifer. "How are you two doing?"

"Hell, Jackie, we are not doing. There is no doing. We went beachcombing. Had a couple of lunches together."

"Ask her to go for a walk. Go over to Campobello Island and take her to Lower Duck Pond. It's beautiful this time of year. Sandy beaches, trees, an absolute paradise."

"Look, Ann Landers, I'm not sure I should."

"Why?"

"Because even though I may have misread the situation, there obviously is someone in her life. Too many people, too much complication." Kristan kept her voice low but drew out each word.

"Uhm. Do you still like her?"

"Don't do that." Kristan was irritated.

"Do what?"

"The wise guru routine. I'm not in the mood."

"I'm being patient, and you're being petulant. You said she'd be a good person to know."

"Yeah, she'd be a good person to know." Kristan sulked.

"Then ask her to go beachcombing again on Saturday. You like her, leave it at that. Besides, the weather will be perfect, and what a place to talk about life."

"Life. Is that what you talk about when you go beachcombing?"

"Of course," Jackie said, studying Kristan over her half-moon glasses. "It's a prerequisite. You can't be on a beach and talk about anything else. The ambiance, the mood—it's all there, talk about life."

"Life." Kristan laughed.

"You know, hopes, dreams, aspirations, love interests, God, religion, but not politics. Wrong place for politics."

Kristan laughed again. "Okay, okay. Can we get off this subject if I ask her to go beachcombing?"

"Agreed."

"I'll ask, okay?" Then Jackie's words sank in. "Right, love interests—" Kristan said in exasperation. "As if I would ask."

"Ask." Jackie offered with a smug smile.

Chapter 20

Thank God it's Friday, Kristan thought. It was the state's last day, Francis had assured her as they entered the courtroom. Kristan was anxious for it to begin. Toby was late.

The first person called to the stand was Billy's friend, Clayton Jones.

Clayton testified that he and Billy were at his home earlier that day working on his car. He said David Robinson showed up with a six-pack, and the three of them had some beers. Then Billy left.

Jones said that after Billy and Robinson left, he continued to work on his car. When he ran out of grease, he said, he went to Billy's house and borrowed some. When he got there, the children were already in the car and Billy said they were headed for Hamilton Cove to have dinner at Burger King.

"Were all the children wearing seat belts?" Jennifer asked.

"Yes."

"Did Billy seem drunk or impaired any way?"

"Absolutely not."

"What happened?"

"Billy told the kids to wait, and he went into his garage and came out with a grease gun."

"Then what happened?"

"He said he'd see me later, and he left."

"Did you ever see them again?" Jennifer asked.

"No," Jones said quietly.

Kristan moved over in her seat to make room for Toby. He was writing already in his notebook as he sat down.

Under Heater's cross examination, Jones admitted that Billy regularly used alcohol, but he denied ever having seen Billy drunk.

Kristan looked over at Tina. She didn't know what she had expected but was somehow not surprised to see no change in her demeanor.

A key witness, Kristan realized after he began to testify, was Danny Green. He said he had been with David and Jerald the day of the accident. Green, a student at the local college, said Robinson was driving because McCormick had told him he did not have a driver's license. He said he had watched Robinson as he popped several pills and washed them down with beer. He admitted they had smoked a lot of marijuana.

Kristan sat back. At last, the silver bullet, she thought.

"What happened next?" Jennifer said in that quiet style she had cultivated for the courtroom.

"David was driving fast and really hitting the drugs hard. I wanted out. I told them I was going to dinner with friends and asked him to drop me off."

"Did he drop you off?"

"Yeah, at Tippys."

"What time was this?"

"Five-thirty p.m."

"How can you be certain?"

"Because I had promised some friends I would meet them for dinner at Tippys at six and I didn't want to be late." Danny paused. "Plus," he said, clearly embarrassed, "I had the munchies."

"How much marijuana did you smoke?"

"We shared two or three joints."

"And how much do you think David Robinson smoked?" Jennifer asked.

"I object." Heater was on his feet. "He is being asked to speculate."

"Counselor?" The judge looked at Jennifer.

"Your Honor, I am just trying to establish the quantity that Mr. Robinson ingested just before the accident. I suspect he may have bragged about how much he had ingested that day."

"Overruled, you may answer the question."

"Like I said, the three of us shared two or three joints, but he bragged about more."

"Bragged?"

"Yeah, he told me he had been smoking pot and popping pills since eight that morning."

"Did he drop you off?"

"Yes, at Tippys."

"And when they pulled away, who was driving?"

"David Robinson," Danny said quietly.

"Have you been with David Robinson before when he was drinking, popping pills and smoking marijuana?"

"Yes."

"When?"

"A couple of times over the past month. He'd pick me up at school or he and Jerald and I would go to a party or something."

"In those instances, when you were in a car, who drove?"

"David."

"Not you or Jerald?"

"Never."

"Never?"

"David never let anyone drive his car. He was proud of that big Chevy, called it his mean machine."

"No further questions, Your Honor." Jennifer sat down.

"Counselor?"

"Danny, you weren't with David all of the time?" Heater said.

"No."

"So you don't know if he let Jerald McCormick or someone else drive, when he was with them. At other times."

"Well—"

"Just answer the question, yes or no."

"No."

"No further questions."

Jennifer was on her feet. "Danny, when you started to say well, what did you plan to say?"

"I object. Relevance?"

"Your Honor," Jennifer said quietly, "Mr. Heater opened up this line of questioning, and I would like to see where his answer takes us."

"Overruled. Witness is instructed to answer the question."

"All I was going to say was that I wasn't with him at all times, but David made it clear that no one else drove his car, and the times I saw him around town in his car and with other people, he was always driving."

"Thank you, Danny. No further questions."

"Counselor, do you have any more witnesses to call?" the judge asked Jennifer.

"The state rests, Your Honor."

"Given the lateness of the hour and the weekend, I think we'll end court now. We'll begin at eight. Monday morning with the defense's case," the judge said as she stood up.

"All rise," the bailiff ordered.

"Not bad," Toby said as he stuffed his reporter's notepad into his jacket. "I think she's got a hell of a case."

131

"Agreed." Kristan glanced at Jennifer. Several people had congregated around Jennifer, and Kristan waited for the group to break up. Although she knew she was pushing her deadline, she waited for Jennifer to look her way.

"Hi." Jennifer continued to push papers into her briefcase. "What did you think?"

"Good." Kristan sought Jennifer's eyes. "Very good."

Jennifer seemed discouraged. "But I haven't put him in the driver's seat just minutes before the crash."

"Close enough."

"Close only counts in horseshoes," Jennifer offered cynically.

"You busy tomorrow?" Kristan asked.

"Just planned to crash."

"No preparation, no study, right?"

"Right."

"Would you like to go beachcombing again? With me?" Kristan said hesitantly.

"I—"

"Don't say no. According to a doctor friend of mine, it's therapeutic. Good for the soul, she says."

"Well, I guess my soul could use a recharge."

"Good. I know a beach on Campobello Island where your soul will be absolutely rekindled."

Jennifer paused, her slim hand on her closed leather briefcase. "Okay." She shook her head. "I'll take you up on that. What time?"

"Well, in anticipation of your saying yes," Kristan said with a grin, "I checked and low tide is at nine a.m. I can pick you up at, say, eight-thirty?"

"I could meet you."

"Nope. I am not going to let you change your mind. You need this, counselor," Kristan persisted.

Jennifer finally looked Kristan in the eyes. "Agreed."

Chapter 21

It was Monday again and Kristan knew she needed to get a move on in order to get to court by eight a.m. The judge offered no reprieve from the rigid time schedule she had set for trial.

Kristan thought about the weekend. It had been wonderful. They'd talked for hours about everything. Although she reached for the telephone all weekend to call Jennifer just to talk, she stopped herself. The train was on the fast track, and she was uncertain where they were going. She spent Saturday night reading.

Sunday, she returned to the beach but felt restless for the first time in years. She walked for hours, studying the shoreline. It amazed her to see the amount of erosion that had taken place in the ten years she had lived there. Just off to the left of where the bench sat, the pounding surf was already cutting a new inlet. It had been only three to four feet deep when she first spotted it: now it was six to eight feet deep.

As she walked into the courtroom, Jennifer made eye contact with Kristan, a small acknowledgment of what they had shared over the weekend. But within seconds her attorney's mantle was in place, and she was a study in concentration.

When the trial resumed, Heater presented Robinson's defense, trying to show that although he was there, he had not been driving.

His first witness was Lee Bradley, who Kristan knew was Robinson's girlfriend. She testified that they were together just hours before the accident and had neither drunk beer nor smoked marijuana. But under Jennifer's skillful cross examination, Lee tripped up on the times and admitted she was at a friend's house at the time she had claimed she was with Robinson. "I'm having trouble remembering the time. I'm just nervous," she told Jennifer.

"What's the deal?" Toby whispered to Kristan. "She's lying."

"She loves him, and she's trying to give him some kind of alibi," Kristan whispered back.

"When you went out with David Robinson, did he always drive?" Jennifer asked.

"Always," Lee said. "He was proud of his car."

"So the times you were with him, he never let anyone else drive?"

Lee stopped; her eyes sought Robinson. "Well, yeah, there were times."

"Lee, a few seconds ago you said he always drove."

"Well, I was nervous."

"You seem to be nervous a lot. No further questions." Jennifer sat down.

Heater next called Robinson's father to the stand. He told the judge that his son and Jerald McCormick had been at their home on the morning of the accident, but he had not detected the odor of alcohol around them. He said they had not behaved as though they were intoxicated.

Heater then waltzed several technical witnesses through who talked about the use of marijuana and how it would impact an individual's behavior. If Heater had hoped to score any points with the judge, Kristan thought, he had failed.

Then David Robinson took the stand. Kristan sat back. She was surprised at this turn of events. But the minute Robinson began to testify, she was not surprised at his cocky attitude.

He testified that he could recall everything that led up to the accident, including drinking a few beers earlier that morning with Billy and their friend Clayton. He denied that he was driving at the time of the accident, said he had become tired and had let McCormick drive.

He claimed he had clear recall of everything he did before the accident, and he said his friend Danny had lied about the drugs and alcohol.

Jennifer continued to hammer him about the drugs he had used, but he was adamant.

She pressured him, forcing him to backtrack on answers he had given. Robinson became belligerent. Kristan watched as his attorney shifted uncomfortably in his seat. Kristan was not surprised. Under pressure, Robinson reverted to the macho bravado that seemed to always get him into trouble.

He finally admitted that he had drunk more beer and smoked a joint, but continued to deny that he had taken barbiturates.

"Then how did the barbiturates get in your system, David?"

"It was probably a mix-up at the lab. Jerald was popping pills, not me. Popping pills when he was driving. He smashed into Billy's car, not me," Robinson announced smugly.

"Wait a minute. Just seconds ago, you said you didn't remember anything that happened. That you and Jerald were talking and the next thing you remembered, your car was on fire and you were standing in front of it. That's what you testified to just minutes ago."

"Right."

"You also testified that you can't remember what happened just minutes before the collision, right?"

"Right."

"Then how do you know that Jerald smashed into Billy's car?"

David looked uneasily at his attorney. "That's what all those people said."

"What people?" Jennifer asked quietly.

"The cops, those people." His manner had turned sullen. He sat sideways in the chair so that when he looked up at Jennifer, Tina was not in his view.

"No, David. All we know is that the accident took place at the fog line and that your car was not in its lane. We don't know who smashed into whom. No further questions, Your Honor." Kristan thought she detected just a tiny grin as Jennifer turned back to the prosecutor's table.

"David." Heater was on his feet even as the words came out of his mouth. "Were you driving at the time of the accident?"

"No, sir, I was not." Robinson raised his head smugly.

"No further questions, Your Honor, and the defense rests," Heater added.

"We'll take a half-hour break. Are you both ready with closing arguments?" the judge asked the attorneys.

"Yes, Your Honor," the two said almost simultaneously.

Kristan fumbled with her notepad.

"You waiting?" Toby asked.

"Yeah. It's not worth my time to go back to the office for a thirty-minute wait. You want to get a Coke?" Kristan asked him. She noted that Jennifer already had left the courtroom, along with Francis.

"Sure."

Toby and Kristan chatted about the trial as they walked to the sandwich shop in the basement of the courthouse.

"I think I struck out," Toby said after they were seated. He studied his Coke.

"How so?"

"I asked Jennifer out. I thought we could go for a boat ride. She asked if you would be joining us. I told her I hadn't asked you. She said it might be nice if the three of us could go out for an afternoon sometime. She danced right around the suggestion of a date."

"Sorry." Kristan squirmed in her seat. She hesitated, uncertain how much she wanted to reveal.

Toby sipped his Coke. "She is genuinely nice. I don't think there has been a glimmer of interest from the beginning, but I was hoping. She's warm and bright, intense at the right moments."

"Oh?"

"You know what I mean."

"Yes, I do," Kristan said with a laugh. "Maybe sometime the three of us could go out on the boat. I'd like that."

"I think she's lonely and would like some friends. I think she and I could be friends as long as I back off on the date stuff."

"How do you feel about that?"

"Okay, really. I'm attracted to her, but the feeling isn't mutual. That was pretty clear."

Kristan glanced at her watch. "We'd better get back."

She stood up and looked at her friend. "Toby, I'm really sorry. I know you kinda dug her, sorry it didn't work out."

"Me too." Toby paused, about to say something and then stopped.

Kristan looked at him, prepared for the question she saw in his eyes, but he said nothing more as they walked back to the courtroom.

Jennifer's closing argument was as organized as the rest of her case. She restated significant points of the case and reminded the judge of the testimony that placed Robinson behind the wheel of his car.

Heater's closing argument was flashy—a lot of loud words, pacing back and forth in front of the judge's bench. He would stop to show a diagram or talk about an aspect of drugs. But for the most part, his argument wasn't any more enlightening than his case.

"The fact is, Your Honor, a tragedy has occurred here. Five people are dead, but let's not compound that tragedy by putting the wrong man in jail," Heater said.

The judge looked at the clock. "I know it's late, but I am going to rule on this tonight." She stood up. "Court is adjourned for two hours."

Kristan shoved her notepad into her back pocket. "Gee, she's going to really push it. I've got to go," she said to Toby. "How about a drink afterwards?"

"You're on," he said he as he too hurried toward the door. "Three Sisters?"

"Great." Kristan ran across the street to her office.

At the office, she quickly brought her editor up to date on the day's events. Said her lead would be the judge's decision, but she would write everything else in preparation for the late hour. "Well, I won't be here. The night editor is Robin."

Ah! Kristan thought. How would she ever be able to live without Jerry's warm guidance? "That's okay. I figure she'll have us back in court by six-thirty. It should take about twenty minutes for her to outline the why of her decision."

"Will she sentence him?"

"Unlikely; the A.D.A. will probably call for a presentence report."

"What's that?"

"Probation puts it together. Talks about his attitude, remorse, if he has any. What kind of sentence Probation and Parole is recommending. Those kinds of things."

"Can you get a copy of that?"

"Unlikely. It's confidential."

A while later, Kristan finished up her story and looked at the clock. It was six-fifteen. The court clerks had not called, so the judge still was in chambers. She longed to call Jennifer but decided against it. She looked at her lead again on the screen. It was a game she played. She always wrote the lead, but left open the option to change it if necessary.

In this instance, it said, "A thirty-year-old Bailey's Cove man showed little emotion Monday, when he was found guilty of multiple counts of manslaughter in connection with an automobile accident that killed five people, including a father and his three children."

If the decision went the other way, Kristan knew all she would have to throw in was found "not" guilty.

A tapestry of tension draped the courtroom when Kristan returned. Family members sat huddled together, quietly talking.

She watched as the court clerks and jailhouse staff, who ordinarily weren't in the courtroom, filed in for the judge's decision. She also noticed that the jail administrator was in the courtroom. Kristan frowned. His appearance usually meant that someone was going to be arrested. Several other deputies also had quietly entered the room dressed in street clothes; Kristan could see their guns bulging underneath their coats. This much court security meant the judge expected her decision to provoke a reaction, possibly a violent one.

Toby had slipped in quietly next to her on the bench. "You see what I see?" He whispered. Toby nodded toward the cops.

"Yeah. Robinson is going down."

"All rise."

Kristan rose to her feet along with everyone else. She realized she was holding her breath.

The judge quietly ticked off each point, her reasoning closely paralleling the points Jennifer made during her closing argument. She scrolled the screen of her laptop as she detailed the eyewitness testimony, including that of Danny Green.

"He convinced me that David Robinson was drinking, smoking and popping pills just one half-hour prior to the accident. And he also was very convincing in his analysis of David Robinson's personality and his need to drive." The judge paused to again look at her notes. "His testimony was reinforced by statements made by the toxicologist about the level and amount of alcohol and marijuana in the defendant's system just before the accident." The judge looked from Robinson to his attorney. "Please stand." The two rose to their feet. Kristan watched Robinson as he avoided eye contact with the judge. "Although we do not have an eyewitness who puts you in the driver's seat at the time of impact, it was clear to this court, not only from the testimony of others, but from your own, that you were the only one driving at the critical moment when the two cars collided," the judge said.

Kristan heard the gasp and saw Robinson's mother clutch her mouth.

"I therefore find you guilty on all counts." She then ordered Robinson be held without bail in the Jefferson County jail pending a presentence report.

It's over, Kristan thought. She looked over at Tina, who met Kristan's gaze with tears in her eyes. Her family, a buffer of protection, escorted Tina from the courtroom.

Kristan glanced at the clock. The pressure was on to get her story sent. Then she would head over to Three Sisters. Tonight she needed a drink.

Kristan tried to reach Jennifer several times at her office, but there was no answer. She had a few minutes before she would walk over to Three Sisters and wasn't surprised when she heard steps in her hallway.

"I tried to call you, counselor, to offer my congratulations."

Jennifer stood with her hand on the doorknob. "Thanks, and I came to thank you for pushing me into taking it to trial."

"Aw, I suspect that in the end you would have come to that same decision."

"We'll never know." Jennifer looked Kristan in the eye.

Kristan could feel her blood pressure crawling up toward the boiling point. "I'm forty-three, eleven years older than you," she blurted.

"I know."

Kristan was dumbfounded. How did she know?

"You forget, reporter, you're not the only one privy to confidential information."

Kristan grinned and scratched her ear. "Some of us are going out to Three Sisters tonight to have a drink. Would you like to join us?"

"Yes, but not tonight. I have a bunch of telephone calls to make, and then I am going to take a long, quiet hot, hot bath."

"That sounds inviting." Kristan stopped, embarrassed at what she was suggesting.

"It is, and no, I don't take it that you are inviting yourself." Jennifer laughed in a free and abandoned way that had Kristan grinning from ear to ear, with a very hot face.

"I'd like to take you to dinner sometime to celebrate," Kristan offered.

"I'd like that, but I want to invite you to my house Friday night for dinner and a small celebration. That's why I stopped by."

"Wait, I've been to your house. I'd offer to cook, but I don't want to kill you, so let me take you to dinner."

"Next time."

"Next time," Kristan agreed.

"This time, I'd like to cook dinner." They agreed on a time, and Jennifer said, "Have fun with your friends tonight and hey, have a drink for me, okay?"

"Okay."

Jennifer left as quietly as she had arrived. Kristan waved her notebook in front of her face. Either the change of life had set in early and had thrown Kristan's heating system into high gear, or she was burning up with desire. Somehow, she knew it was the latter. She almost decided to forgo the drink in favor of a cold shower.

⬥⬥⬥

The bar was noisy. It was adult volleyball night, and nearly everyone she knew was there. Kristan glanced around looking for Toby and found him off to one side, talking with several members of the volleyball team.

"Hey, I hear he went down the tubes," the community development director yelled at Kristan from across the bar.

She just grinned and waved.

Music was screaming in the background from the jukebox, and Kristan realized that as she got older, loud music seemed less attractive.

"Hey," she greeted Toby, "let me buy you a drink."

"Sure."

Kristan made her way to the bar. She waved to Jessica who was standing behind the bar, making drinks as fast as she could. "One Budweiser and the usual," she yelled.

"Sure thing."

"I bet you're glad its over," Jessica said, the din of the music making her have to speak directly in Kristan's ear.

"Yeah."

"Go the way you thought?"

"It went the way it had to," Kristan said.

Jessica set two drinks in front of Kristan, and Kristan pulled out a five-dollar bill and tossed it on the counter. She waved away the change.

"I am glad it's over," Toby said as she put the beer in front of him.

Kristan squeezed the lime that Jessica had dropped into her seltzer, then dropped the twisted peel into the ashtray. She wiped her hands together, her fingers smelling of lime. "Me too."

"I saw Jennifer going into your office. Anything important?" Their chairs were pulled close together so they could hear each other.

"Naw, she's just glad the trial is over."

Toby leaned back against his chair. He looked around the bar and smiled at several of his friends. He tugged at his unshaved chin. "You like her?"

Kristan shrugged.

"When I threw out the challenge months ago, my ego said I was the one who would win, but I have a feeling the best man won." He bit his lower lip, trying to hold back a grin.

"I'd say woman," Kristan shot back at her friend. "I didn't mean for this to happen."

"I know. At first I was pissed. Then I decided I might not understand it, but I can't change how . . ."

"Some women feel about some women?"

"Uhm."

"That's pretty sensitive on your part."

"Hey, just because I'm a man doesn't mean I can't be sensitive to what's going on around me. Kristan, I saw how you looked at her. It was not how you ordinarily look at the women around here."

"I'll have to be more veiled in how I look at women in the future."

"Naw. I doubt most people notice. I noticed but that's because I also was attracted to her."

"Well, my friend, I'd say we both have good taste in women." Kristan clinked her glass with Toby's.

"You two going to get together?" Finally the music had turned to a soft rock song. Kristan turned back to the bar, and Jessica gave a quiet wave of acknowledgment. She had slowed down the tempo of the music.

"Don't know. There are several complications in her life."

"Friends?" Toby held up his beer.

"Always."

143

Chapter 22

Jennifer stood in the shower, the hot water pushing away the stress of the day. It had been several days since the trial had ended, and she felt good. The water splashed over her skin, flowing past all those wonderful crevices and streaming down her legs. She scrubbed the bar of soap over her breasts and down her stomach.

She smiled as she recalled her aunt's saying about hurried bathing. "Wash up as far as possible and down as far as possible and let possible go until tomorrow." But tonight, Jennifer spent extra time on possible.

She stepped out of the shower and glanced at the clock on the wall in her bathroom. She had fifteen minutes to dress.

The spaghetti sauce had cooked for hours; she would put the pasta on when Kristan arrived. The antipasto was ready and cooling in the refrigerator. Jennifer slipped into a white oxford blouse and jeans. Since she was at home, she chose bare feet.

She hummed a nondescript tune and stopped to think about her first autumn in Cranberry Bluffs. The fall colors were a harmony of reds, yellows and browns and they contrasted spectacularly with the blue ocean. She loved living in a picture postcard. She was pleased because her parents planned to spend September with her. She wanted Kristan to meet them.

She heard the car in the driveway even before she saw the outdoor electric eye kick on the outside light. She sighed. There would be no interferences tonight. She had left her beeper in the bedroom and hoped Kristan had left hers at home. She opened the door before Kristan knocked.

Kristan looked up in surprise, her curled knuckles still within reach of the door.

"Hi. Come in."

"Hi." Kristan handed her the wine and flowers.

"Thank you." She sniffed the flowers. "I love flowers." She smiled and headed into the living room.

Kristan could smell the Oscar de la Renta and thought she was going to melt. She decided lesbians must have a heightened sense of smell. Or at least this lesbian did, she thought, because she felt her knees wobble as she trailed behind Jennifer.

"No excuses this time?" Jennifer smirked. "No murder, no mayhem?"

"No." Kristan felt her blood pressure rise.

"I hope you're hungry."

"Starved. I was in Bayport all afternoon watching the construction on the new port."

"Good. I'm starved also, but how about some wine to warm you up and . . ." Jennifer gestured toward the woodstove in the living room. ". . . a warm fire."

"Yes to both," Kristan said. "Can I help in the kitchen? I'm pretty good. I can do more than just dishes."

"Nope, everything is nearly ready. I just have to pour us some wine, put the flowers in water, and I'll start the pasta after we've had our drink. Just relax." Jennifer smiled.

Kristan gulped. She felt as if she was in the vortex of a tornado—calm, but the storm of passion just a fingertip away.

They had talked on the telephone several times since the trial, their conversations dancing just on the edge of intimacy. She had promised herself she would not ask Jennifer any questions about Pam. She stood near the fire, her hands extended, the warmth radiating over her. She felt Jennifer's presence even before she turned around.

Jennifer handed her one of the wineglasses. "To friendship." She reached her glass out to touch Kristan's.

"To friendship." Kristan smiled. "I know how your week was, but I hope you are planning a restful weekend."

"Yes." Jennifer gestured Kristan to a chair. "As you know, Robinson is to be sentenced in two weeks. One week before Labor Day."

"Any guesses on what the judge might give him?"

"Hard to say. But how about we not talk shop tonight?"

"Agreed." They shared a small silence as they sipped their wine.

"You like being a reporter?"

"Oh, so we are going to talk about my shop," Kristan said teasingly, her manner comfortable. "Most of the time."

"What do you like most?"

"Well, I learn something new almost every day. That may seem like a weird thing to like, but I do. When you're a general assignment reporter, you become a baby expert on almost everything."

"Baby expert?"

"Yeah, like all the stuff about marijuana and the THC Delta Nine that you had the expert witnesses talk about during David's trial. I know just enough to write about it, but I'm no expert."

"I wasn't either until that case." Jennifer hesitated, then rubbed her hand across her forehead. "I'm just glad it's over."

"Me too."

"And I have you to thank."

"Not really. You'd have come to the same conclusion yourself," Kristan said again. "I didn't do anything."

Jennifer leaned forward and touched Kristan's arm. "I wonder if I would be thanking you now if I had lost. I guess we'll never know." Her eyes were sultry.

Kristan felt the hand on her sleeve, the small hand with the long angular fingers that sent sparks up her arm.

Jennifer stared at her. "I want to kiss you."

Kristan swallowed. "I want to kiss you too. In fact I've been fantasizing about it."

"Fantasy is no substitute for reality," Jennifer said as she leaned forward. Her lips were open, inviting exploration. "Kristan, you have to meet me halfway." Jennifer's eyes mirrored the inside of a blast furnace, hot, molten, burning.

With one fluid motion, Kristan's wineglass was on the table and her lips were on Jennifer's. She reached out to touch Jennifer's softness. She buried her mouth against Jennifer's neck. "I am not going to be able to stop."

Jennifer pulled Kristan's mouth back to hers. "Don't," she said against her lips.

Kristan unbuttoned Jennifer's blouse with one hand while her other hand reached down to pull Jennifer's hips into her. She inhaled sharply when she saw the red bra that stood as a sensuous invitation to what lay underneath. Kristan did not want to rush. She let her tongue trace a line just above where the bra met Jennifer's skin.

Jennifer moaned softly, deep in her throat. She tugged at Kristan's shirt and then pulled it over her head. No bra. She gently cupped Kristan's breasts. "I want to feel you against me," she said to Kristan's throat. Her arms went up and around Kristan's shoulders as Kristan pulled her tightly against her. Kristan felt the softness of the bra against her nipples and gasped as she sought out Jennifer's mouth for a long searching kiss.

She heard Jennifer's moan as her hand caressed her skin. She kissed Jennifer's shoulder, her lips again following that same slow path down to the soft place between Jennifer's breasts. She pulled her onto her lap.

"I've wanted to taste them from the moment I met you." She reached behind, unhooked the bra and eased the straps over Jennifer's shoulders.

Kristan's hair felt like a feather on Jennifer's skin as Kristan's lips and then her tongue did a slow circle around Jennifer's nipple and finally drew it into her mouth. Jennifer reveled in the teasing tug of Kristan's lips. She drew to her knees as Kristan continued to feast on her breasts. She kissed the top of Kristan's head, then tilted her head back and kissed her mouth with an intensity that demanded a response.

Kristan's fingers stroked Jennifer's back, beginning at her shoulders and slowly moving downward, then eased her back against the couch. Her tongue traveled down and under Jennifer's breast, tracing a warm path to her belly where she stopped at the top of her jeans.

"I want to taste everywhere." Kristan's voice smoked with desire. She slowly unzipped Jennifer's jeans. Her tongue followed the slow movement of the zipper downward. She hesitated when she saw the red lace bikini panties that matched the bra. "This is like opening a magnificently wrapped gift," she said. Her tongue stroked the skin just above the coarse curly hair, then she kissed her way back up Jennifer's belly, then to her breasts. She sucked first one and then the other. She touched the outside of Jennifer's jeans and Jennifer arched her body against Kristan's hand.

"I can't do it with my jeans on."

Kristan massaged Jennifer with the heel of her hand and Jennifer matched the rhythm. Suddenly she felt the first wave of orgasm overtake over. She pulled Kristan's mouth hard against hers, then lay back panting. "That was a nice surprise." She smiled, her eyes inviting more.

"Just the beginning." Kristan again kissed the skin just above her pantyline.

"Please, take them off." Jennifer squirmed as she pushed at the top of her jeans.

Kristan leaned back on the sofa and eased the jeans and panties over Jennifer's hips, and pulled them away from her feet. Jennifer sank deeper into the couch. "Let's go to bed." Jennifer whimpered.

"Later." Kristan's breath felt hot against Jennifer's thighs, and her tongue darted across and behind Jennifer's knees tracing a circular pattern. Jennifer bit her bottom lip in anticipation of the climb upwards to the spot where all her pleasure seemed focused.

Jennifer arched as she felt Kristan's tongue on and in her. It traced a large circle around Jennifer's wonder spot, momentarily touching it and then pulling back to continue the circular motion. Jennifer reached forward and grabbed Kristan's hands as they gripped her thighs. "Please. Do it now."

Kristan returned to that magical spot between Jennifer's legs and focused on those tiny nerves.

"Oh, yes," Jennifer said between clenched teeth.

Kristan lifted Jennifer's hips, her tongue and lips sucking in Jennifer's passion. Jennifer's body began to react, and suddenly Kristan felt her tighten against her.

As Jennifer began to relax, she felt Kristan slip inside her. She could not believe how hot those fingers felt as they probed the inner places of her being. As the movement intensified, her body, almost independent of her mind, began to match the rhythm of Kristan's hand.

The rhythm intensified. Kristan's hand moved faster and Jennifer met each of her thrusts. Jennifer pushed down and stopped, and Kristan lay over her as the climax shuddered through her.

Jennifer pulled Kristan's face against hers. "So good," she said against her lips.

"What about the spaghetti?" Kristan said, her breath warm against Jennifer's neck. "You were starved."

"I still am," Jennifer said as she rose up and eased Kristan over onto her back. "Let's have it for breakfast."

Then she began her own slow, passionate exploration.

Chapter 23

Kristan set the glass of wine on her table and sat back in her easy chair. Although the red light on her answering machine was blinking with a number of messages, she ignored it. She could still smell Jennifer on her clothes and in her skin. The woman had touched every inch of her body during their marathon lovemaking.

She could still feel the exhilaration. She could see Jennifer's intense look and the way her lips opened just before they kissed. She pressed fingers against her lips and they felt wonderfully bruised.

She remembered the way Jennifer's hands played over her arms and breasts, and she recalled the way Jennifer gasped just before her orgasms. She had never been with a woman who made love so intensely. Kristan rubbed her hand over her chest and felt a sudden warmth between her legs.

The telephone rang, but she just ignored it. This time there was no message. It was Sunday night, and she had to think about going back to work Monday morning. A knock at her kitchen door jarred her thought patterns. She was unaware of her surroundings. The house was dark; she had not bothered to turn on a light when she had arrived home. She hadn't even turned up the heat, but she had not felt cold.

Kristan saw Jackie's outline through the curtain. "Hi," she said as she opened the door.

"Hi yourself. You okay?" Jackie stayed on the porch.

"Yes." Kristan stepped back. "I'm sorry, come in."

Jackie critically looked at Kristan. Kristan could feel the hot flush creep up her neck and into her cheeks. She broke eye contact and turned away.

" 'Would you like a drink, Jackie?' " Jackie said, taking on Kristan's hostess duties. " 'Well thank you Kristan, I'll . . .' "

"Okay, okay." Kristan held up her hands to stop the dialogue. "I'm having a glass of wine." Kristan poured her a glass and led Jackie into the living room. She gestured for Jackie to sit. "What?" she said defensively, trying to break Jackie's silent stare.

"You in love?"

"I don't know, but I do know I'm not ready to talk about it yet. Agreed?"

"Agreed. I wanted to let you know that everyone else is. Your car was in her driveway for two days, for God's sake. You could have at least taken a break and moved it around the corner. Everyone noticed and they're all clucking about it."

"Damn small towns." Kristan shook her head in frustration. "I wasn't exactly thinking of moving cars."

"Well, no one will ask you any pointed questions, but you'll probably be teased."

"No doubt." Kristan smiled. "She is an incredibly exciting woman," she said, more to herself than to her friend. "But there still is that problem." Kristan frowned at her half-glass of wine. "The other woman."

"I know, but . . ."

"But?"

"Has Jennifer said what she wants?"

"I don't think she knows, but I knew what I was getting into, so if there is any damage to my psyche, it was voluntary masochism."

"That's a tough one. I had hoped Jennifer would resolve that before you two got involved."

"Yeah, well, we got involved, as you say, and things are not resolved." Kristan studied the tops of her shoes. "I have to stay focused here. It was an incredible two days, and I know up here"—Kristan pointed at her head—"that I could fall desperately in love with her. But for now, I've got to treat this as just a moment, a once-in-a-lifetime moment that you're glad you had."

"Look, my little friend, why not fight for her?"

"I don't see that there is any forum to fight in." Kristan stopped Jackie's protest. "I'm here and she's not, but Jennifer and the other woman have a lot of history. Besides, I'm not sure what I can offer her. Jacks, I'm not sure what I want. It's been so many years since I have lived with anyone. Can I do that cohabitation thing? That's what I have to think about."

"If she's the right woman, it will be the only thing you want."

"Look at me!" Kristan stood up, her frustration growing. "This self-contained person that I have worked to create is coming unhinged. My psyche is as deformed as one of those blobs from outer space movies. I feel as adrift as a jellyfish."

Had her pain not been so raw, Kristan knew that Jackie would have laughed at the imagery, but thankfully she kept her expression unchanged.

The ring of the telephone interrupted them. Kristan sat back in her chair. Her first instinct was to ignore the telephone, but Jackie's presence made her feel guilty. She reached for the telephone. "Hello. Oh, hi," she said softly. It was Jennifer.

Jackie smiled, got up and started toward the kitchen. "I'll wait in here."

❧

"You can come back," Kristan called shortly. "She said I should tell you thank you."

"For what?"

Kristan offered a sheepish grin. "I told her you were the one who suggested the two beachcombing days."

"When do you plan to see her again?"

"We're going out to dinner Wednesday night. That's my first free night. I have meetings Monday and Tuesday." Kristan lapsed into thought.

Jackie finished her wine and stood up. "Look, I know you want to be alone to bask in that afterglow of lovemaking, but think hard, my little friend. If you really like her she just might be worth the fight."

Kristan stood up and hugged Jackie. "I'll think about it." They walked back through the house and toward the back door. "Thanks for being so sensitive. I'm not sure I would have read the same signs." Kristan stopped. "You know about wanting to be alone. You are one cool friend."

Jackie kissed Kristan on the cheek. "And you are one special lady."

Kristan watched Jackie climb into her red Mustang She turned and leaned against the kitchen door. For the first time in years, she hated the thought of getting into bed alone.

Chapter 24

Kristan resisted the urge to hug Jennifer when they met in the parking lot. Jennifer had called earlier in the day and asked to meet her at the Shoreside Inn. Kristan was disappointed, but she heard something in Jennifer's voice and agreed.

"I know you probably already are on top of this," Jennifer said after they had been seated at a corner table. "But Robinson is scheduled to be sentenced a week from today at ten a.m."

Two days before Labor Day, Kristan thought. "Thanks." Kristan folded her hands and placed them on the table. "But that's not why we're here instead of some place private."

"No. Are you always this direct?"

"'Fraid so. Comes with the territory."

"Well, I like it most of the time." Jennifer toyed with her water glass, then took a sip. "I'm leaving for Portland Friday night."

Kristan quashed the emotional response that was whirling inside her.

Jennifer leaned forward, her fingers just inches from Kristan's. "I need to resolve the past before I can focus on the future."

Kristan didn't respond.

"You're not going to make this easy, are you?"

"Jennifer, I don't know what to say. I knew the risk and took it, but I'm not going to herald your departure with brass horns. I don't want it," Kristan said softly. "But I also know I don't get a vote."

"I feel like my life has been a picture puzzle since I've been here. I keep adding pieces to this puzzle, my job, what happened between you and me, friendships, but . . ." Jennifer gestured toward the imaginary puzzle. ". . . but down here in the corner, there are these missing pieces." She paused. "The pieces to my future. And I can't fill in those pieces until I resolve all that emotional baggage I brought here from Portland."

"Will she persuade you to go back to her?"

"She's very persuasive."

"We've never talked about why the breakup." Kristan stopped as Maggie Stanley walked toward them. "Ladies, can I interest you in a drink?"

"Wine?" Kristan looked at Jennifer.

"That would be nice."

"Do you have a preference?"

"No, go ahead and order."

"Maggie, bring us a carafe of white zinfandel. We haven't even looked at the menus, so give us a few more minutes."

"Sure." Maggie reached for the pitcher of ice water that sat nearby and refilled Jennifer's glass.

"We've never discussed why you broke up," Kristan repeated.

"Pam is a very charismatic personality. I'm sure you've met women like her, people are just drawn to them like—"

"Flies to a manure pile?" Kristan said with ironic humor.

"Well." Jennifer laughed. "I guess you could characterize it that way, but I doubt Pam would see herself that way." Jennifer paused as Maggie returned to the table and set two glasses on the table. She poured just a small amount into one glass. Kristan gestured for her to fill the glasses. "I can't do that wine-tasting thing, Maggie. You know that's just too pretentious for Jefferson County."

"I agree," Maggie said softly to Kristan. "But the boss wants it. Says when the tourists come in here that's what they like."

"Well, we're not flatlanders. By the way, I am ready to order," Kristan said without looking at the menu. She knew that she could not prolong the evening without losing her cool. "I'll have the haddock with lobster sauce, rice pilaf and the house dressing on my salad."

Jennifer gave her a quizzical look. "I'll have the same," Jennifer offered. She waited until Maggie left. "Want to get out of here?"

"I can't see the sense of making this any harder than it needs to be," Kristan said quietly. "Anyway, you were telling me about Pam."

"We don't need to talk about this."

"Oh, but I think we do. Pam is unfinished business and until you resolve it, well . . ."

"The first time she cheated on me we weren't living together. It was an older woman in the office where she had been hired as a law clerk. We resolved that."

"Very understanding of you."

"Or just plain stupid." Jennifer sipped her wine. "The second time it was a woman attorney she had met from another firm."

"And you resolved that?"

"It was during the second year we lived together. We broke up, but she promised it would never happen again."

"But there was a next time."

"Yes. You would wonder how someone as bright as I am could keep stepping back into that manure pile you described. Anyway, three things happened at once. My grandmother died, leaving me the house here. We were just going to use it as a summer retreat, a getaway place. Then I found out she was—" Jennifer gestured. "She swore that it was nothing more than two friends getting together. That they had not been intimate. But something broke, and I realized that there would always be something like that. When the job opened up with Francis, I didn't just jump at it, I leapt with heart, body and soul."

"But you're going back."

"Yes."

Kristan saw Maggie approach out of the corner of her eye. She sat back in her chair and rested her hands in her lap. Maggie set salads in front of them, refilled their wineglasses and left. Kristan smiled to herself. Maggie must have sensed the earnest conversation, otherwise she would have stayed and chatted.

"Do you love her?"

"I'm not certain if it's current love, or the nostalgia of old love. When I left Portland I was hurt and angry."

"When do you expect to be back?"

"Late Sunday night."

Kristan cut her salad into smaller pieces. Her brain was racing. Where would Jennifer stay? Kristan set her knife down and chewed thoughtfully on her salad.

"Can I ask you a question?" Jennifer broke in.

"Sure."

"Why did you and your ex break up?"

"I fooled around on her. She kicked me out, as she should have," Kristan answered.

"Is she . . . ?"

"No, she moved away several years ago. She got a teaching job at a university in Massachusetts."

Jennifer set her fork down and studied Kristan. "Do you do that?"

"I did that," Kristan said. "Once."

"Maybe you have more in common with Pam than—"

"Whoa, lady. I had been in a ten-year relationship. That does not excuse what I did, but—oh, I can't even explain it." Frustration

157

tinged Kristan's voice. "Anything I say now about that time sounds like just an excuse. I did it, I regret it, I haven't found anyone until recently"—Kristan looked at Jennifer— "that I would even want to think about having a future with."

"Is that what you are thinking about, a future."

"Yes." Kristan held her breath.

"I'm glad, because that's what I've been thinking about. That's why I have to go back now, not later."

"But don't do this because of me." Kristan wanted to reach over and take Jennifer's hand in hers. To stroke the same fingers that had aroused such passion in her. Instead, she pushed her unfinished salad aside and drank her wine.

"After last weekend, I was hoping there was more than just the physical attraction, but frankly you are so self-contained, so sure of your space, I didn't think there was room for anything else in your life."

"Jennifer, there isn't room for anything else in my life as long as you have a past to contend with. I am not going to allow myself to fall in love with you only to have you announce six months or a year from now that you are going back to Portland, or worse, that Portland is moving here."

Jennifer smiled. "I like how you refer to Pam as Portland. Maybe that's what I have to contend with—the geography, not the person."

Kristan frowned.

"No, I'm not being flippant."

Maggie approached with their food. "The plates are hot, so be careful. Can I get you anything else?"

"I'm fine." Kristan looked at Jennifer. "We're fine. Thanks, Maggie."

"I'm beginning to think my idea of choosing a public restaurant wasn't such a good idea," Jennifer said. "I did it because I didn't want to lose all this talk in some kind of emotional—"

"It's funny," Kristan interrupted. "When you first suggested going out to dinner, I wanted to be someplace alone with you, but

158

this was the right choice. Not one that makes me happy, but the right choice."

"Thank you." Jennifer appeared shy.

"I have to be mature about this," Kristan began. "That contrasts sharply with what I want to do."

"And that is?"

"Bury my mouth in your neck, feel you against my body. Feel how you—"

Jennifer asked suggestively, "You want to leave?"

"No. Yes, but no. I want this over and you back here with me but—" Kristan leaned her chin on her thumb, her index finger resting against her lips. "If that doesn't happen, I will survive. My friend Jacks said I should fight for you, but I don't think that's what you want. I think only you can decide this."

"We've never talked about love. I know I could fall deeply in love with you."

"It's my charm," Kristan offered flippantly. "Sorry. Unfortunately I use that kind of humor as a linguistic crutch. I want to talk about love, Jennifer, but not now. It would hurt too much later."

"I want to see you before I leave."

"I can't." Kristan pushed her hand through her hair. She could feel her depression growing. "All I ask is that you give me the answer as soon as you get back. Promise you'll call me Sunday night, regardless of the time and regardless of the answer."

"I promise." Jennifer toyed with her plate, her fork pushed the half-eaten fish aside. "I know this is good, but I honestly don't feel very hungry."

"Let's go. Maggie, could we have the check?"

Maggie looked from Jennifer to Kristan. "Kristan, is there something wrong with the fish? If there is, I'll send it back and get you whatever you want."

"The fish is great," Kristan said, reaching for her wallet. Jennifer had already gone to the coatroom. "We're just not very hungry."

Kristan looked at the bill and threw two twenties and a ten on the table.

Jennifer stood outside in the cold September night. Her collar was pulled up around her cheeks. "Look at all those stars," she said as soon as Kristan had joined her.

"Fall nights are so spectacular here." Kristan didn't know what to say to cover the awkwardness she felt.

She turned toward Jennifer and took her in her arms. "I'm not going to kiss you," she whispered in her ear. "But I am going to ask you to come back." Jennifer buried her face in Kristan's neck. Kristan could feel her warm breath on her skin; her knees began to tremble. She released Jennifer and turned away, her keys ready; she jumped into her car. She could not look back.

Chapter 25

For the rest of the week, Kristan managed to avoid Jennifer. She purposely stayed away from the places she might be. She even skipped the arraignment of a man who was charged with arson. She lied to her assignment editor and told him she had forgotten the date. Jerry was not happy, but Kristan reminded him that it was the first time she had ever forgotten an important court date.

Jackie had called several times and wanted to talk, but Kristan was not ready. When Jackie asked her to go for a hike on Saturday, Kristan told her she planned to clean house. It was the only excuse she could fashion and her intentions had been good. She had planned to clean house.

Kristan knew Jennifer had left for Portland at around four p.m. Friday.

She struggled through Friday night, watching mindless television. Saturday morning she had awakened early only to lie in bed and think.

At noon on Saturday, although she had promised herself to do a full morning of housework, she was still in her chair, sipping chocolate milk and staring at the fire. It was definitely an opera-listening day. She had loaded the CD player with Maria Callas and other opera favorites. "*Mild und Leise*" from Wagner's *Tristan und Isolde* was playing, and Leontyne Price was throwing her into an absolute state of depression.

"I knew it." Jackie walked into the room. Kristan could hear the frustration in her voice. Jackie snapped off the amplifier.

"What the hell are you doing?" Kristan demanded, raising herself from the chair.

"Saving you from a day of dreary self-pity."

"I want self-pity." Kristan fell back into the chair.

"No damnit. Come on." Jackie took Kristan's hand and easily pulled her from the chair.

"What is this, you barge in here, pull me out of my chair?"

"It gets worse, my friend. Get dressed," Jackie ordered, her hands firmly on her hips. "Or I will dress you."

"You will not."

"Oh yes, I will." Kristan, always alert to Jackie's tone, heard the promise in her voice.

"Shit, Jackie, just leave me alone."

"No, we are going to go beachcombing, and then tonight you're coming over to my place for dinner, and tomorrow—"

"Hold it. I'll go beachcombing and tonight I will have dinner with you, but that's it. Really, I'll be okay. I just have to get through this—whatever it is going on in my head." Kristan turned away, holding back the tears. "I never thought anyone could get that close to me again. Jacks, thanks for being here."

"Come here." Jackie held open her arms.

Kristan buried herself there. She felt the warmth of trusted comfort envelop her.

"It's a good thing no one locks doors around here, or I would have had to bust my way in," Jackie said.

162

Kristan laughed and wiped her eyes. "And I don't doubt that you would have."

"Well." Jackie looked down at her size-ten boots. "It would have been hard, but I'm up for a real Clint Eastwood-type rescue. Now go get dressed. It's cold out."

Kristan followed Jackie down the trail to the ocean. They walked up and over the cliffs across the beach to Boot Cove where there were more high cliffs to climb. "Come on, let's sit. I'm younger than you and I'm pooped." Kristan laughed. She brushed sand off a large rock and pulled herself up on it, and sat cross-legged. Jackie's presence was a comfort. There were no questions. "You know what's strange about all of this?"

"What?"

"Jealousy. I am feeling such unbelievable jealousy right now, I could scream." Kristan rested her elbows on her knees, her head in her hands. "I don't even want to think about what they could be doing right now." She bit at her bottom lip. This was a new emotion and she was uncertain how far she would go before she did scream.

"If I were where you are, that's what I would feel."

"Really? But it seems so illogical."

"Why illogical?"

"Because I have nothing to be jealous of. She hasn't made any promises. We had one weekend, she has been honest and straight-forward. So why do I feel jealous?"

"Because you want more of what you had, and you can't stand to think of her sharing that with someone else. But, Kristan, you don't know that she is. I would trust Jennifer. I haven't even met her, but I know you, and I know the kinds of people you trust and I think that whatever happens, Jennifer will come back here to resolve the situation with you before she hops into bed with what's-her-name."

"Pam. I hate the name. Pretty childish, huh?"

"Yeah, but at times like this we can give in to those childish irrational moments. It works, for a while."

"Jacks, can I ask something?"

"I think I know what it is. About Marianne."

"In all the years you were together, did you ever think to, you know." Kristan gestured helplessly.

"Yeah. There were temptations."

"Did you?"

"No. And not because I'm such a wonderful person. You have to remember, Marianne and I found each other later in life. I was your age, in fact, she was two years older. It was like coming home. She was everything I wanted—a great lover, a wonderful companion, a brilliant mind. She challenged me. There was no more room in my life for anything or anyone else. I wanted to go home at night."

"You're lucky. Luckier than most. I don't think many people find that level of happiness, contentment."

"We were not unique, but I agree it seems like everyone we know, straight and gay, is coming apart. Divorces and separations seem so much more common now."

Kristan drew her finger through the sand on the rock. "Even if Jennifer comes back, I don't know what she wants, or what I want. Maybe I just don't want to get my hopes up and begin thinking about a future only to have it dashed with—"

"All you can do is wait."

"That's what I am not good at. I think that's why I found it so easy to be a reporter. I want to make things happen. I don't wait for people to call me. I call them. I push and probe to get a story, but in this instance, I don't know what to push or probe. I feel impotent. All I want to do is sit and stare at a wall and listen to music." Kristan could feel the cold seeping through her down jacket as the fall sun began to dip.

"Come on, I'm cold." Jackie pulled her to her feet. "I don't have any answers. My specialty is the body, not the mind, but I do know that your being alone right now is not a good thing. Come on, we're going to go pig out on chicken wings and potato salad and watch a terrible old movie. Something silly like *Going My Way*, or better yet, *The Bells of St. Mary's*. That's what you need—some mindless Bing Crosby romantic suds."

Kristan enjoyed the day, and sitting through *Going My Way* had been pure escapism. Before she left Jackie's house, she had promised she would return Sunday morning for breakfast. They were going to watch some more old movies.

When Kristan got home she bypassed the stereo. She had promised Jackie there would be no more melancholy music. She had made a lot of promises in the past twelve hours.

She stripped out of her hiking gear and decided that a shower would help her relax before bed. She heard the loud knocking, and she pulled her sweatpants and a T-shirt back on and frowned at the bedroom clock. Who the heck would be at her door at midnight?

If she walked slowly enough down the stairs, she thought, maybe they would go away. She knew it wasn't Jackie, because she had said she was headed for bed. Other friends knew to call before they came over. The knocking continued until Kristan switched on the outside light and opened the door.

Jennifer was in her arms before she could speak. Kristan crushed Jennifer's body against her own, her coat cold against her arms. "Tell me this is permanent," Kristan said against her mouth.

"Yes. As permanent as you want it. If you want me."

"Want? Want? I am in want of you. I want to ask who, what, where, when, why." Kristan kissed her lips, her cheeks, her eyes. "But."

"Tomorrow." Jennifer gently pushed her back into the kitchen. All Kristan could think of was that she was glad she had declined Jackie's offer to spend the night at her house. As Jennifer closed the door with one hand and pulled her jacket off with the other, she whispered, "For now, I just want to make love to you."

Chapter 26

Kristan found herself back in court, Toby to her right, Marcy to her left. The television crew had lined their cameras up along the side wall.

Kristan and Jennifer had been inseparable since her return from Portland.

"Been busy?" There was a smirk just below the surface in Toby's question.

"Yeah, too busy to even have a beer with her friends," Marcy said. Amusement did a jitterbug in her eyes.

"I don't want to be teased." But Kristan knew her protest sounded more fancy than fact.

"I'm surprised she got here today." Marcy raised an eyebrow at Toby. "Heard she hasn't spent a lot of time in a vertical position."

Kristan blushed and looked away. She wished court would start, but she knew that was an idle wish, since neither Jennifer nor Francis was in the courtroom yet. The sheriff's deputies had not brought

Robinson over from the jail, either, so until the cast of characters was assembled she would be the subject of a lot more teasing.

"You two—" Marcy stopped when she saw the door to the attorney's room open and Jennifer and Francis step out. Jennifer looked over at Kristan, flushed and quickly looked away. Kristan felt her heart go into overdrive, she felt wet where she should have been dry.

"Ah, love." Toby had not missed the look.

Kristan's face and ears were burning, her temperature just below boiling.

"Yeah, ain't it great?" Marcy offered.

Kristan slid lower in her chair. She stared at her notebook.

"When's the wedding?" Toby asked.

"That's it." Kristan felt a strangled noise emanate from her throat. "No more." She looked over at Jennifer who just smiled. That woman is cool, Kristan thought. They had not been together last night because Jennifer had to prepare for today, but Kristan looked forward to tonight. Jennifer looked rested, her face relaxed.

Kristan's attention was drawn to Tina and her family as they entered the courtroom. Kristan's eyes sought Tina's, but she would only stare at the floor. She had tried to talk to her after the trial, but Tina had pulled her protective cloak even closer around her. Her mother had said that Tina kept anyone and everyone who reminded her of the accident away. Kristan knew she would have to wait.

Robinson's family was already in the courtroom. There was a quiet buzz of conversation, but it all stopped when two deputies escorted Robinson in, his attorney trailing behind him.

"He's lost weight," Marcy whispered to Kristan.

"He's going to lose more weight before this is over," Kristan said.

"All rise," the bailiff said as he held open the courtroom door for the judge.

Judge Margaret McDermott took her seat. "Be seated," she said, then nodded at Jennifer. "Proceed."

Jennifer again related the sequence of events on the night of the accident. She talked about what she believed a fair sentence would be. She said it was up to the court to study the criminal code and sentencing options. She also asked the court to consider letters from family and friends and listen to their statements.

The sentencing issue, Jennifer said, was reduced to one question: "What is the appropriate sentence to impose upon an individual who operates a motor vehicle at a very high rate of speed on a major public way, while under the influence of a combination of marijuana and intoxicating liquor with a dose of downers thrown in, and as a consequence of his reckless actions, kills five people?"

Jennifer said that those unlearned in the law could easily decide that the maximum sentence of forty years would not be enough. The answer, she said, was that there had to be proportionality of sentencing and even those who kill intentionally and knowingly are not sentenced to life in prison in Maine.

But, Jennifer argued, the court had enough sentencing room, up to forty years, to structure an appropriate sentence for someone who killed five people.

Kristan was overwhelmed with Jennifer's delivery. The words were soft, the delivery gentle, but underneath lay an intensity. An intensity Kristan had felt when they made love. Kristan sighed. She had to concentrate on Jennifer's words.

Heater argued that Robinson was not a danger to the public, and because there was a question over his guilt, a long sentence would not be fair. He reiterated his contention that the fatal crash was simply a terrible accident. He told the judge that he believed the only fair sentence would be probation.

After Heater finished, the judge stared at her hands for a long moment, before she spoke. Kristan watched her carefully. Except for glancing at a few notes, the judge spoke extemporaneously.

She talked about other cases and the number of years given to those defendants. She talked about proportionality in sentencing and what a judge would like to give, versus what the state would allow. She cited a case where a man, driving drunk, had killed a woman and her baby and had received a five-year sentence. In another case, she said, a man driving while under the influence had killed two teenagers, and he was given forty years. The Maine State Supreme

Court had overturned that sentence, claiming it was excessive. She talked about other cases where the sentences ranged from seven to fifteen years.

The judge paused. "Please stand," she said, and Robinson and his attorney rose. "In all my years as a judge, I have never seen such incontrovertible proof that someone who claims he was not driving really was. You were driving, Mr. Robinson. And although you can stand here and deny that, the facts presented by the state demonstrate, at least to my mind, beyond a reasonable doubt that you were responsible for the deaths of all of those people. Your denial," she continued, "demonstrates that you are not ready to accept responsibility for what you have done. Although I would like to add years of time to your sentence because of that denial, the law prohibits me from doing that. What I can do is fashion a sentence that keeps you off the roads and away from society for at least some time." Judge McDermott paused. "It is without any reservation or hesitation that I sentence you to fifteen years in prison, with all but twelve years suspended."

"No," Robinson's mother said. One of the sheriff's deputies moved in the direction of his family.

"I also sentence you to concurrent sentences of fifteen years, with all but twelve suspended on the other charges."

Kristan did a mental calculation. Robinson got fifteen years in prison. With good time he'd be out in eight.

The judge rose, and the bailiff was calling for everyone to get to their feet.

"What do you think?" Marcy asked Kristan.

"I don't know." Kristan frowned. "I just don't know." She looked toward Jennifer, who had not moved from her seat.

"I gotta go. I've got to send this," Kristan said to Marcy and Toby. "I'll meet you guys later at Three Sisters."

Kristan looked toward Tina. Her family had formed a circle around her. They were leaning over, talking to her. Tina's mother, Mary, was wiping tears from her eyes. A lump welled up into Kristan's throat. Get me out of here before I lose it, she told herself.

Chapter 27

It felt so right walking on her beach with her arm around Jennifer. There was something about it that was absolutely seductive. Jennifer had draped her arm around Kristan's waist and she marveled at how well their bodies meshed both in and out of bed.

It was a warm fall morning, Maine's Indian summer. An eagle was circling overhead, its sharp eyes attuned to their movements but clearly more interested in watching for a scurrying creature that would serve as lunch.

She thought about the warm and fuzzy glow she had felt when she awoke earlier that morning next to Jennifer. She was surprised at how easily she had adjusted to having someone else so close to her. She had nestled her nose against Jennifer's hair and slid her arm around her waist.

"Isn't it wonderful how two people can make love most of the night and wake up wanting to make love?" Jennifer said sleepily.

"I was hoping." Kristan snuggled closer and caressed Jennifer's breasts.

"Good. I like it when you lead the dance."

"Isn't that a bit femme for such a modern woman?"

"Uhm. But sometimes it's nice to just follow."

Kristan kissed Jennifer's neck. Her lips and tongue glided across to her ear. Jennifer shivered. "That feels wonderful."

Kristan had then rolled Jennifer onto her back and moved on top of her, feeling the full length of her body. She had marveled at the excitement she felt just touching Jennifer.

As they walked on the beach, Kristan shivered at the memory.

"What are you thinking about?" Jennifer asked.

Kristan pulled her into her arms and kissed her lightly on the nose. "I was thinking about how wonderful it is to wake up next to you. This is the way life should be."

Jennifer had an amused look on her face. "It is wonderful isn't it." She snuggled into Kristan's arms. "Aren't you afraid to be seen nuzzling a woman in public?"

Kristan put her head back and laughed. "I own two miles of beach. The only one who is watching is that eagle, and he only wishes we were small enough to be his lunch." Kristan leaned forward and rested her head against Jennifer's.

"Why the scowl?" Jennifer asked.

"We have to talk."

"Uh-oh, I feel a practical attack coming on. Okay. Let's talk, but let's walk while we do it. This feels so right."

"That's what we have to talk about. Jennifer, this feels so right."

"Look." Jennifer stopped and turned toward Kristan. "You've been alone for so long, I am not going to place any demands upon you. You have to tell me what you want."

Kristan's eyebrows knitted. "I want you on whatever terms you want. If you want to live together, then we'll live together. If you want to spend half your time here and half your time at your place,

171

that's fine. But what I don't want is for this to be a one-weekend moment. I love you. I am in love with you."

Jennifer sighed. She pulled Kristan closer to her. "All I thought about on my trip to Portland was how I was driving away from you, and it made me realize that all I wanted to do was drive back. I had fallen in love with you. I'm not certain when that happened, but—"

"It's my charm. It has a way of invading your pores, sneaking into your gray matter. I'm not surprised you succumbed so easily." Kristan lightly ran her fingers across Jennifer's back and felt her shiver.

Jennifer shook her head. "Am I really going to have to get used to this editorial bravado shit? I think we need a bit of an ego adjustment here. I think the lady who was bowled over by a certain woman's charms was you."

"You're right. I can't believe how fast I fell for you." Kristan scowled again. "Actually, I was scared. I haven't felt that way in so many years. Scared that you wouldn't come back, scared that if you did, then—"

Jennifer placed a single finger over Kristan's lips. "I know. But I'm here, and I love you. I don't want to answer the question about living arrangements yet. I like my house. I like yours. During the renovations to my house I'll stay here, but after that maybe we'll have a week and weekend home. I just know this is right, and the rest will follow. But I do know what I need," Jennifer said. "A commitment."

"What kind of a commitment?"

"Not a 'till death do us part' thingie, but an agreement that it'll just be you and me as long as we are together. I can't ever deal with a someone else in your life."

"Very lawyerly—'thingie.'" Kristan feigned speaking to an unseen judge. "'Your Honor,'" she said in a low voice. "'The state wishes to argue that one Kristan Cassidy on a beautiful September morning entered into a thingie of her own free will and now is attempting to break that thingie.'"

Jennifer's teeth pulled at her bottom lip. "I expect I am going to have to get used to this humor?"

Kristan turned serious. She touched Jennifer's cheek. "I love you, and I am not going to fool around on you, it took me too long to find you. But I am not going to ask for the same promise from you." Kristan shifted her arm and reached a hand up to stroke Jennifer's hair. "You are a gift. And for as long as you want to be here, I will treasure that gift."

Jennifer put her finger against Kristan's lips. "I love you. I can make that commitment. I don't want anyone else, now or in the future. So there will be no one-sided contract, Ms. Reporter, or 'thingie.' I want you for however long it lasts."

Kristan leaned over and kissed Jennifer. Her tongue sought out the warm mouth that only hours earlier had given her so much pleasure. *A lifetime is what I want,* Kristan thought as she began to stroke Jennifer's back, *for however long a lifetime there is.* "You know, I've never made love to anyone on this beach."

"Aren't you afraid we might get sand on us?"

"Not if we're creative."

"I get the feeling that life with you is going to be an adventure," Jennifer said as her lips returned Kristan's kiss.

About the Author

Diana Tremain Braund continues to live on the coast of Maine in a house that overlooks the water. She and her dog Bob, who is now six-years-old, take long walks on the beach. That is where she comes up with ideas for Bella Books. You can email the author at dtbtiger@yahoo.com.

Publications from
BELLA BOOKS, INC.
The best in contemporary lesbian fiction

P.O. Box 10543, Tallahassee, FL 32302
Phone: 800-729-4992
www.bellabooks.com

SUBSTITUTE FOR LOVE by Karin Kallmaker. One look and a deep kiss… Holly is hopelessly in lust. Can there be anything more? ISBN 1-931513-62-7 $12.95

MAKING UP FOR LOST TIME by Karin Kallmaker. 240 pp. When three love-starved lesbians decide to make up for lost time, the recipe is romance. ISBN 1-931513-61-9 $12.95

NEVER SAY NEVER by Linda Hill. 224 pp. A classic love story… where rules aren't the only things broken. ISBN 1-931513-67-8 $12.95

PAINTED MOON by Karin Kallmaker. 214 pp. A snowbound weekend in a cabin brings Jackie and Leah together… or does it tear them apart? ISBN 1-931513-53-8 $12.95

THE WAY LIFE SHOULD BE by Diana Tremain Braund. 173 pp. With which woman will Jennifer find the true meaning of love? ISBN 1-931513-66-X $12.95

GULF BREEZE by Gerri Hill. Could Carly really be the woman Pat has always been searching for? ISBN 1-931513-97-X $12.95

THE TOMSTOWN INCIDENT by Penny Hayes. 184 pp. Caught between two worlds, Eloise must make a decision that will change her life forever. ISBN 1-931513-56-2 $12.95

BACK TO BASICS: A BUTCH/FEMME EROTIC JOURNEY edited by Therese Szymanski—from Bella After Dark. 324 pp. ISBN 1-931513-35-X $12.95

SURVIVAL OF LOVE by Frankie J. Jones. 236 pp. What will Jody do when she falls in love with her best friend's daughter? ISBN 1-931513-55-4 $12.95

DEATH BY DEATH by Claire McNab. 167 pp. 5th Denise Cleever Thriller. ISBN 1-931513-34-1 $12.95

CAUGHT IN THE NET by Jessica Thomas. 188 pp. A wickedly observant story of mystery, danger, and love in Provincetown. ISBN 1-931513-54-6 $12.95

DREAMS FOUND by Lyn Denison. Australian Riley embarks on a journey to meet her birth mother . . . and gains not just a family, but the love of her life. ISBN 1-931513-58-9 $12.95

A MOMENT'S INDISCRETION by Peggy J. Herring. 154 pp. Jackie is torn between her better judgment and the overwhelming attraction she feels for Valerie. ISBN 1-931513-59-7 $12.95

IN EVERY PORT by Karin Kallmaker. 224 pp. Jessica's sexy, adventuresome travels.
ISBN 1-931513-36-8 $12.95

TOUCHWOOD by Karin Kallmaker. 240 pp. Loving May/December romance.
ISBN 1-931513-37-6 $12.95

WATERMARK by Karin Kallmaker. 248 pp. One burning question . . . how to lead her back to love?
ISBN 1-931513-38-4 $12.95

EMBRACE IN MOTION by Karin Kallmaker. 240 pp. A whirlwind love affair.
ISBN 1-931513-39-2 $12.95

ONE DEGREE OF SEPARATION by Karin Kallmaker. 232 pp. Can an Iowa City librarian find love and passion when a California girl surfs into the close-knit dyke capital of the Midwest?
ISBN 1-931513-30-9 $12.95

CRY HAVOC A Detective Franco Mystery by Baxter Clare. 240 pp. A dead hustler with a headless rooster in his lap sends Lt. L.A. Franco headfirst against Mother Love.
ISBN 1-931513931-7 $12.95

DISTANT THUNDER by Peggy J. Herring. 294 pp. Bankrobbing drifter Cordy awakens strange new feelings in Leo in this romantic tale set in the Old West.
ISBN 1-931513-28-7 $12.95

COP OUT by Claire McNab. 216 pp. 4th Detective Inspector Carol Ashton Mystery.
ISBN 1-931513-29-5 $12.95

BLOOD LINK by Claire McNab. 159 pp. 15th Detective Inspector Carol Ashton Mystery. Is Carol unwittingly playing into a deadly plan?
ISBN 1-931513-27-9 $12.95

TALK OF THE TOWN by Saxon Bennett. 239 pp. With enough beer, barbecue and B.S., anything is possible!
ISBN 1-931513-18-X $12.95

MAYBE NEXT TIME by Karin Kallmaker. 256 pp. Sabrina Starling has it all: fame, money, women—and pain. Nothing hurts like the one that got away.   ISBN 1-931513-26-0 $12.95

WHEN GOOD GIRLS GO BAD: A Motor City Thriller by Therese Szymanski. 230 pp. Brett, Randi, and Allie join forces to stop a serial killer.   ISBN 1-931513-11-2 $12.95

A DAY TOO LONG: A Helen Black Mystery by Pat Welch. 328 pp. This time Helen's fate is in her own hands.
ISBN 1-931513-22-8 $12.95

THE RED LINE OF YARMALD by Diana Rivers. 256 pp. The Hadra's only hope lies in a magical red line . . . climactic sequel to *Clouds of War.*   ISBN 1-931513-23-6 $12.95

OUTSIDE THE FLOCK by Jackie Calhoun. 224 pp. Jo embraces her new love and life.
ISBN 1-931513-13-9 $12.95

LEGACY OF LOVE by Marianne K. Martin. 224 pp. Read the whole Sage Bristo story.
ISBN 1-931513-15-5 $12.95

STREET RULES: A Detective Franco Mystery by Baxter Clare. 304 pp. Gritty, fast-paced mystery with compelling Detective L.A. Franco   ISBN 1-931513-14-7 $12.95

RECOGNITION FACTOR: 4th Denise Cleever Thriller by Claire McNab. 176 pp. Denise Cleever tracks a notorious terrorist to America.   ISBN 1-931513-24-4 $12.95

NORA AND LIZ by Nancy Garden. 296 pp. Lesbian romance by the author of *Annie on My Mind.*
ISBN 1931513-20-1 $12.95

MIDAS TOUCH by Frankie J. Jones. 208 pp. Sandra had everything but love.
ISBN 1-931513-21-X $12.95

BEYOND ALL REASON by Peggy J. Herring. 240 pp. A romance hotter than Texas.
ISBN 1-9513-25-2 $12.95

ACCIDENTAL MURDER: 14th Detective Inspector Carol Ashton Mystery by Claire McNab. 208 pp. Carol Ashton tracks an elusive killer.
ISBN 1-931513-16-3 $12.95

SEEDS OF FIRE: Tunnel of Light Trilogy, Book 2 by Karin Kallmaker writing as Laura Adams. 274 pp. Intriguing sequel to *Sleight of Hand.*
ISBN 1-931513-19-8 $12.95

DRIFTING AT THE BOTTOM OF THE WORLD by Auden Bailey. 288 pp. Beautifully written first novel set in Antarctica.
ISBN 1-931513-17-1 $12.95

CLOUDS OF WAR by Diana Rivers. 288 pp. Women unite to defend Zelindar!
ISBN 1-931513-12-0 $12.95

DEATHS OF JOCASTA: 2nd Micky Knight Mystery by J.M. Redmann. 408 pp. Sexy and intriguing Lambda Literary Award-nominated mystery.
ISBN 1-931513-10-4 $12.95

LOVE IN THE BALANCE by Marianne K. Martin. 256 pp. The classic lesbian love story, back in print!
ISBN 1-931513-08-2 $12.95

THE COMFORT OF STRANGERS by Peggy J. Herring. 272 pp. Lela's work was her passion . . . until now.
ISBN 1-931513-09-0 $12.95

CHICKEN by Paula Martinac. 208 pp. Lynn finds that the only thing harder than being in a lesbian relationship is ending one.
ISBN 1-931513-07-4 $11.95

TAMARACK CREEK by Jackie Calhoun. 208 pp. An intriguing story of love and danger.
ISBN 1-931513-06-6 $11.95

DEATH BY THE RIVERSIDE: 1st Micky Knight Mystery by J.M. Redmann. 320 pp. Finally back in print, the book that launched the Lambda Literary Award–winning Micky Knight mystery series.
ISBN 1-931513-05-8 $11.95

EIGHTH DAY: A Cassidy James Mystery by Kate Calloway. 272 pp. In the eighth installment of the Cassidy James mystery series, Cassidy goes undercover at a camp for troubled teens.
ISBN 1-931513-04-X $11.95

MIRRORS by Marianne K. Martin. 208 pp. Jean Carson and Shayna Bradley fight for a future together.
ISBN 1-931513-02-3 $11.95

THE ULTIMATE EXIT STRATEGY: A Virginia Kelly Mystery by Nikki Baker. 240 pp. The long-awaited return of the wickedly observant Virginia Kelly.
ISBN 1-931513-03-1 $11.95

FOREVER AND THE NIGHT by Laura DeHart Young. 224 pp. Desire and passion ignite the frozen Arctic in this exciting sequel to the classic romantic adventure *Love on the Line.*
ISBN 0-931513-00-7 $11.95

WINGED ISIS by Jean Stewart. 240 pp. The long-awaited sequel to *Warriors of Isis* and the fourth in the exciting Isis series.
ISBN 1-931513-01-5 $11.95

ROOM FOR LOVE by Frankie J. Jones. 192 pp. Jo and Beth must overcome the past in order to have a future together.
ISBN 0-9677753-9-6 $11.95

THE QUESTION OF SABOTAGE by Bonnie J. Morris. 144 pp. A charming, sexy tale of romance, intrigue, and coming of age.   ISBN 0-9677753-8-8 $11.95

SLEIGHT OF HAND by Karin Kallmaker writing as Laura Adams. 256 pp. A journey of passion, heartbreak, and triumph that reunites two women for a final chance at their destiny.   ISBN 0-9677753-7-X $11.95

MOVING TARGETS: A Helen Black Mystery by Pat Welch. 240 pp. Helen must decide if getting to the bottom of a mystery is worth hitting bottom.   ISBN 0-9677753-6-1 $11.95

CALM BEFORE THE STORM by Peggy J. Herring. 208 pp. Colonel Robicheaux retires from the military and comes out of the closet.   ISBN 0-9677753-1-0 $11.95

OFF SEASON by Jackie Calhoun. 208 pp. Pam threatens Jenny and Rita's fledgling relationship.   ISBN 0-9677753-0-2 $11.95

WHEN EVIL CHANGES FACE: A Motor City Thriller by Therese Szymanski. 240 pp. Brett Higgins is back in another heart-pounding thriller.   ISBN 0-9677753-3-7 $11.95

BOLD COAST LOVE by Diana Tremain Braund. 208 pp. Jackie Claymont fights for her reputation and the right to love the woman she chooses.   ISBN 0-9677753-2-9 $11.95

THE WILD ONE by Lyn Denison. 176 pp. Rachel never expected that Quinn's wild yearnings would change her life forever.   ISBN 0-9677753-4-5 $11.95

SWEET FIRE by Saxon Bennett. 224 pp. Welcome to Heroy—the town with more lesbians per capita than any other place on the planet!   ISBN 0-9677753-5-3 $11.95